OPERATION RACEHORSE

THE MYSTERY OF THE USS ELDRIDGE DD213

MIKE DIXON

www.writeandreleasepublishing.com

TABLE OF CONTENTS

PART ONE

Chapter 1   FIRST IN A SERIES 3

Chapter 2   I'M NOT A FAILURE..................................... 14

Chapter 3   HASTE MAKES WASTE 24

Chapter 4   URGENT 28

Chapter 5   THE REUNION 33

Chapter 6   RIDERS IN THE SKY..44

Chapter 7   LIFE GOES ON 48

Chapter 8   THE HORSES ARE IN THE GATES 51

Chapter 9   THIRD AND FINAL IN A SERIES.................54

Chapter 10   SOMETHING WENT WRONG.....................62

Chapter 11   SEPARATE WORK FROM PLAY 69

Chapter 12   HEADING FOR HOME 74

Chapter 13   AND THE WINNER IS.................................81

PROLOGUE

WORLD REVIEW LITERATURE

For one to create such a masterpiece—one that dares to encompass the entirety of human existence—would require firsthand experience of the extraordinary. And yet, such an achievement is not just implausible, not merely unthinkable, but entirely impossible.

Or, as this great work compels us to ask: What if it isn't?"

MARY HEATH

WORLD REVIEW LITERATURE

BERLIN, GERMANY - 1925

The science lecture hall was calm and still. An unearthly quiet prevailed. There was a palpable tension in the air, thick with anticipation. Gathered were scholars, researchers, and men of industry; some of the greatest minds of the time. They sat poised, their collective breaths held in a moment of unspoken expectation. A twenty-two-year-old genius stood on the podium, a young man whose very presence demanded attention. He reached into the pocket of his well-worn jacket, pausing for just a second as his dark eyes scanned the audience. Then he smirked, with a knowing, almost mischievous expression, as if he alone possessed the key to a great secret.

He straightened. His voice, though calm, carried across the hall with the weight of certainty.

"Mr. Chairman and distinguished guests—I stand before you with a conscious soul, a full heart, and an open mind. The latter to be the topic of my presentation."

Not a whisper stirred. The room, packed with some of the greatest intellects of the era, hung on his words. Among them sat Albrecht, the celebrated physicist and chemist; Lemeroux, a renowned botanist; Chezinski, the acclaimed archaeologist; and none other than Charles Leaky himself. All were transfixed, leaning forward, eyes unblinking. It was as if they expected not a lecture, but a revelation.

This young man, this Jewish former dropout, was about to introduce an idea that could shake the foundations of science, one that, if true, would change the world forever.

He continued, his voice gathering momentum,

"Reality, gentlemen, is nothing more than a construct of the mind. What we perceive, we shape. What we imagine, we can make real. The mathematical possibilities are endless! And yet, we remain shackled—chained to traditional laws, clinging to outdated limitations."

He paced slightly, his mind racing faster than his words.

"A speck of dust. A fraction of a grain of sand. Do you believe that particles a million times smaller do not exist? They do. And they are a billion times more powerful! The forces of nature exist in triads—threefold systems of energy that, if harnessed correctly, can unlock abilities far beyond what we now conceive as possible."

A murmur rippled through the audience, but no one spoke outright.

"Gentlemen," he pressed on, eyes flashing, "these minute, invisible forces—these 'atoms,' as we call them—will not only illuminate our homes and fuel our future… but when manipulated with precision, they will grant us the power to shape reality itself. And what's more—when combined with other unseen forces of the universe, they will give us the ability not only to win a war, not only to conquer nations but to alter existence itself. And, if misused…"

He paused, allowing his stunned audience a moment to reflect, then continued,

"They will give us the power to destroy all of mankind!"

WEST HILLS HIGH SCHOOL, NOVEMBER 12, 1992

The bell rang, but the students weren't ready to leave.

"Tell us a story D."

Michael Donovan, known to his students as Mr. D, leaned back against his desk, shaking his head with a smirk.

"Tomorrow gang. Tonight, I want everyone to start their homework. Pages 281-282. Do the evens. Copy the sentence, and fill in the blanks with the correct verb. Then, translate each one."

A collective groan swept through the room.

"Mr. D…c'mon man! Translate again?"

"Yeah, Bobby Jo," Donovan said, "If you can speak Spanish, you can get a girlfriend. Someone's gonna have to take care of you someday…like a pretty senorita, Bobby."

Laughter erupted as the kids hooted in unison, playfully nudging Bobby Jo. He shook his head, trying to hide his grin.

"T.J.! That's enough," Donovan said, raising an eyebrow. "No put-downs. Get to work, now!"

"Sorry D…ok, do like the man said…get to work y'all"

Donovan let the laughter settle before nodding toward the door. The students trickled out, still buzzing with energy.

Mr. D. Michael Donovan. High school teacher, five foot ten. Former second baseman for the Kansas City Royals turned Russian linguist, teacher, turned coach. Still fast and strong. Still capable of taking a mean infield and throwing batting practice for hours on end. But he wasn't just any teacher. Or just any coach. To them, he was Mr. D., a mentor, friend, and a protector.
His brown hair, once thick but now thinning, was combed back. Yet, his boyish face had hardly aged, and his brown eyes remained

sharp and full of life. At 2:30, he dismissed his family, as he called them, as he watched them spill into the halls.

Now… where was I?

He flipped open a book, running his fingers over the worn pages. Chekhov. "The Crow," page 77…

"…With general conscription…," muttered Filenkov, "when even professors are taken to be soldiers… when everyone is an equal… and even—"

Donovan let out a dry laugh, shaking his head. "Christ! I used to translate this Russkiy like I downed beers! A word a second!"

He sighed and leaned back in his chair, the memories of the times racing through his head. There were days when he missed it—missed the rhythm of the game, missed the loud "crack" of the bat against a ball, as well as the rush of speaking a language so foreign, yet once so natural.

But here he was.

Teacher. Coach. Something more.

DAILY CALIFORNIAN NEWSPAPER, NOVEMBER 13, 1992

"I don't know Clair. The Padres have a hell of an overhead this year. The big salaries have to go."

Cid Gilmore pinched the bridge of his nose, leaned back in his leather chair, and shifted the phone to his other ear.

"Okay, we'll run it, but it'll stir up the bees. And get that section on *Person Of the Month* on page six please, will you? Alright....bye."

He set the receiver down and exhaled, rubbing his eyes. Another deadline. Another news cycle. Another damn decision that didn't really matter in the grand scheme of things.

His gaze drifted to the photograph on his desk—three young men, sitting on the hood of a military jeep in Kuwait. One of them was him. The other two were A-10 pilots.

They had been shot down by an Iraqi SAM site and spent six days wandering the desert, surviving on two packets of army rations and a couple of canteens of water.

It wasn't Vietnam heroics or some WWII legend, but it was enough for the folks back home to call them heroes.

That's what mattered, right?

THE PAST NEVER STAYS BURIED.

Cid turned from the photo and stared out the window at the Mission Valley traffic below. His reflection glared back at him from the glass, but his mind was somewhere else.

Gangs. Drugs. Bullshit.

He had survived it all.

Made it out of the ghetto. Got into Stanford. Basketball. Football. Journalism.

He had made it.

And then…

His fingers drummed against the desk. His jaw tensed.

Then, the bodies. The burning homes. The stench of death in the streets.

Then, the *thud* of the DC-3 as it took machine-gun fire, the sickening *lurch* of the plane before it went down in the Salvadoran jungle. The fire. The chaos. The smell of fuel and blood.

And the lies. Cid swallowed hard, but the taste of memory wouldn't go away.

"…What the fuck did we do, man?" His voice was barely above a whisper. "What did I do?"

He had gotten out of college and walked straight into a suit and a lie—a slick-talking ex-Nixon crony who fed him bullshit and called it patriotism.

"Just some security reports," they told him. "Just intelligence. You're helping keep the world safe."

Except it wasn't just intelligence. It was a cover-up. And he was the one writing it.

"We'd like you to report on the Agency's efforts to seek out Juan Bautista, the Chilean drug lord," they had said.

Bautista wasn't just some trafficker. He was a funded asset, a cog in the machine, a dirty little secret the U.S. was happy to keep in play as long as the money flowed in the right direction.

Cid clenched his fists. He would never forget that goddamn report.

He never forgot how it felt sitting in a room full of Washington suits and listening to them lie through their teeth while young men died for - MONEY, GREED AND POWER!   "Goddamn CIA bastards!", he bellowed. The words came out bitter and loud. He exhaled, shaking his head, and reached for the half-empty glass of whiskey on his desk and mumbling,

"The past doesn't just haunt you. It owns you."

PART ONE

FIRST IN A SERIES

The alarm clock buzzed.

Donovan woke at his usual 4:00 am, swung his legs over the edge of the bed, and exhaled. Another day, another routine. He brewed his morning coffee, turned on the television, and switched on the weather channel.

"…Fog will prevail over most of the coast this morning, clearing by 10 am. Sunny skies, with light sea breezes and temperatures will be in the mid 70's. Winds will be from the northwest at five knots."

Donovan smirked. "Good, I'll take the boat out today, anchor in the bay, and grade all these exams. Hey, the story of my life!"

A sharp thud against the front door signaled the arrival of the morning paper. Right on time. He was pleased that his phone call to the <u>Daily Californian</u> had guaranteed its delivery at 5:00 am. Besides, he knew the editor. They had been good friends since 1978, when Cid had been a civilian under contract to the Navy, serving aboard the USS La Salle with him during the Iranian crisis.

Donovan paused and remarked, "What are friends for if not to make sure your paper's here by 5:00 a.m.?"

He unfolded the newspaper, his eyes barely grazing the front page before a bold headline pulled him back in time.

"CHARGERS MAKE PLAYOFFS!" the headlines screamed. Donovan leaned back, sipping his coffee as the past came rushing in.

SUNSET PARK, LA MESA— 1995

Donovan's mind suddenly went back to Sunset Park in La Mesa.

As a boy, he and his friends spent hours on the sidelines, watching the likes of Keith Lincoln, Gary Garrison, and Sam Gurniesen going through their daily practice sessions with the rest of the Chargers squad. He still remembered Dennis Partee booting sixty-yard punts into the end zone. Every so often, a stray ball would go awry and soar over the old wooden fence, landing in the thick tangle of ice-plant vines behind a run-down apartment building. That was their cue. Mike and the others would climb the fence and search for the ball. The lucky "shagger" who found the ball would earn a free Coke and an old Charger t-shirt after practice. A prize worth every scrape and bruise.

But to Donovan, the fondest of these memories was of "Bambi", the sleek-footed Lance Alworth. Donovan would wait anxiously on the sidelines, until Sid Gillman, the head coach, blew his whistle, signaling the end of practice.

The moment it sounded, Mike would make a beeline sprint towards his idol, yelling, "Mr. Alworth, can I carry your pads and helmet up, please? Can I?"

A pat on the head would indicate *"yes"*. Donovan clutched the helmet and the huge shoulder pads as if they were treasure. He walked beside his hero, soaking in every second of the short trip to the locker room, feeling like he belonged to something bigger than just being a kid on the sidelines.

And every single time, a gracious Lance Alworth would always have a handshake ready, a "Thanks, kid" and a t-shirt. Mike lived for those moments.

Donovan blinked, stared down at his half-empty coffee cup, and realized he had lost himself in the past again.

"Man, those were the good old days. Fun times. People were people then. When was that? 1965! Long damn time ago!"

Donovan's mind began to ramble even faster and farther away. He finished his customary two cups of coffee, put the paper aside and turned his attention to a yellow pad of paper that was half open and lying on the corner of the marble coffee table.

"Now, let's see. Where was I?"

Donovan began to write a few lines for one of the many short stories he had begun. He was a teacher, but his ultimate dream in life was to be a writer; to write his "Greatest Story Ever Told."

Donovan couldn't keep up with his thoughts, "The second baseman dove to his left, speared the line drive, and flipped the ball to the shortstop. Double play. The crowd went wild!"

For a few seconds, the words flowed effortlessly, the way they always did before reality interrupted. Mike stopped again, distracted this time by several library books piled on his desktop. He glanced at the yet, unread non-fiction books: **The Painted Men**, by T. C. Letherbridge, **Forgotten Worlds,** by Robert Charraux, **The Secret of Atlantis,** by Otto Muck, **From Ghetto to Glory,** the story of Bob Gibson, and, **The Quality of Courage,** by Mickey Mantle.

Donovan began to feel the usual "buzz" from the strong black coffee he always guzzled first thing in the morning. His heart started to pound, and he became impatient. His body was telling him it was time to do his morning workout. He donned his blue-gray sweats, his West Hills baseball shirt and headed out for his morning jog. While he ran, he began to wonder, "What went wrong? Where am I going?" He began to sweat as his heartbeat accelerated to 160 beats per minute. His career-ending knee injury began to ache. "What if? What if I were to become a writer? I like it. Maybe I should quit. Maybe I should leave it all behind. Maybe---"

Just as his imagination took flight, "Ladies and gentlemen, the author of….."

A Ford Ranger's blaring horn startled Donovan back into reality. A familiar voice shouted out, "Hey coach, wanna race?"

It was Jim Shepherd, the school's groundskeeper at West Hills. Mike waved back,wiped the sweat from his brow, and increased his effort as he headed over Mast Bridge toward the high school just a mile away from his two-bedroom apartment.

After a three mile run, an hour of weight lifting, thirty minutes of biking and one hundred sit-ups, Donovan finally called it.

By the time he stepped back into his apartment, sweat clung to his shirt, and his muscles ached—not that he minded. The ache was proof he was still moving, still pushing forward. With a fresh cup of coffee, he settled onto the couch, flipping open the morning's Daily Californian.

Routine. Familiar. Except today, his fingers hesitated. On the table next to it sat the San Diego Herald. The competition. Donovan was loyal to Cid's paper, but the Herald had a section he couldn't resist, entitled, **"You and I"**. It consisted of the following sections;

Profiles.
Letters to the Editor.
Historical Insights
Strange, Offbeat Stories.

Those were special features. The paper was a goldmine of oddities, a reminder that truth was often stranger than fiction.

As Donovan began to scan the headlines, he muttered, "Let's see what we have today"

"MRS. TURNBLOOM'S CHERRY PIES FOR GEORGE WASHINGTON'S BIRTHDAY"…

He smirked. "Now this ought to be great reading!"

Then, his eyes moved to the next headline. "What's this? Okay, now we're getting somewhere…ATOM BOMB OR INVISIBILITY?"

He chuckled, shaking his head. "That's why I love this section. It gets more entertaining every week! People will write anything to be famous!"

But as the last few sarcastic words left his lips, his eyes darted down to the byline. He noticed the author's name who wrote the article. Mike's eyes became wide as saucers. He took a deep breath, but his pulse had already kicked into overdrive. His lips parted as he mouthed the title once again and the author's name, this time with genuine disbelief;

ATOM BOMB OR INVISIBILITY
FIRST IN A FOUR PART SERIES
BY DON STEINMETZ
SPECIAL STAFF WRITER
SAN DIEGO HERALD.

"OH MY GOD! WHY WOULD **HE** BE WRITING SOMETHING LIKE THIS!" Donovan erupted.

His fingers tightened around the newspaper, barely holding it together. His eyes darted back to the article, scanning the text as his heartbeat pounded in his ears.

Whatever this was—it wasn't just another story. It meant something. His gut told him so. And Donovan had learned to trust his gut. He had to keep reading.

He skimmed the first few lines, half-expecting nonsense. But the more he read, the more the words sank in, unsettlingly familiar, " December 3, 1925 – University of Berlin"… He sat up straighter, scanning the text again, this time slower, ".. A stunned scientific community, Einstein, and a radical new theory." The lead was intriguing and Donovan had no choice but to read on…

"From **THE PRUSSIAN YEARS**, a magazine devoted to science and invention, circa 1925", The article began by providing some background regarding some theories on physics…

Donovan kept reading as the words on the page became more profound with every sentence,

"…Did you know that on December 3, 1925, the Father of Relativity stunned the scientific community by addressing two hundred colleagues at the University of Berlin's science lecture hall while casting light on the topic of invisibility?" The article went on.

"Taking a crumpled piece of paper from his tweed coat pocket, a then young, radical and vivacious Dr. Albert Einstein casually, yet boldly, began to explain that "time and space are one and atoms are particles that would someday change the world – for the worse, not for the better." He introduced to a shocked audience that electromagnetic energy and gravity are very clearly related."

He scanned the pages again, his pulse quickening. The article continued,

"Stopping and wiping the sweat from his forehead with a handkerchief, the calm, confident and determined young scientist surveyed his audience and noticed that he did, for the moment, have their undivided attention. Then, with the eloquent arrogance he exclaimed,

"My fellow colleagues, I have developed what will now be called THE UNIFIED THEORY. This in essence, captures the forces of nature in a way that you may, levitate, transport, and make disappear, by a unique way of what I call, IONIZATION-REORGANIZATION or, MOLECULAR REPOSITIONING, the act of actually moving an object of considerable mass – without known

power, make it disappear and then, reappear someplace else. And, with this, comes untold, unforeseen amounts of energy, energy that is derived from moving small particles called electrons, protons, and neutrons. Yes! This will change the history of mankind!"

Donovan got a lump in his throat. He skimmed the words again, slower this time. "Electrons, protons, and neutrons. Yes! This will change the history of mankind!"

He exhaled sharply, his fingers gripping the edges of the newspaper. This wasn't just some sensationalist headline.

It was the past speaking directly to the present—a moment in time that had already happened, one that echoed everything happening now.

A chill went down his spine. He could almost hear Einstein's voice. The hall, the murmur

of a restless crowd—And then, as if the ink itself carried a pulse, the past unfolded before him.

The article continued:

And with this, the lecture hall suddenly burst out in the most unprecedented, yet unexpected sarcastic grumblings, of, *'ah's'* and *'oohs'*. Distinguished men began to mock and heckle Einstein. Then came the comments - blunt, cutting, unforgivable;

'You are simply nuts Albert! You are beyond mad!'

'Lunatic!'

'Atoms? Energy?'

'Why are you wasting our time?'

Distinguished men—respected physicists, chemists, and scholars of the highest order—shook their heads, some laughing outright, others whispering in condescending tones. A few stood, scraping their chairs across the marble floor as they stood and gathered their coats.

A ripple of movement swept through the hall.

Some shook their heads in disbelief, others muttered under their breath, their frustration barely contained.

A few paused—throwing a final disappointing glance at Einstein before turning away.

The exodus began in waves.

Scholars gathered their belongings, adjusted their ties, and walked briskly toward the exits, their voices low but cutting.

"A waste of time."

"I expected more from him."

"The man has lost his mind."

Snide remarks drifted from every aisle displaying signs of dismissal, mockery, disappointment. The last of the elite group disappeared through the grand double doors—leaving only silence in their wake.

Einstein gripped the sides of the podium, his knuckles whitening, but his expression remained calm. His sharp eyes tracked the exodus, watching the last of the great minds file out, their fleeing hanging in the air like smoke.

And yet—

A small, yet comforting smile curled at the corner of his lips. He exhaled, almost amused.

"They'll see," he murmured under his breath.

"They'll find out. It's just a matter of time."

With deliberate ease, he slipped the crumpled notes back into his pocket, as if he no longer needed them. Then, without hesitation, he turned on his heels and strode toward the rear exit— Not defeated. Not broken. But with the quiet certainty of a man who had just shown a glimpse of the future.

THE SECRET HISTORY OF EINSTEIN

My fellow scientific enthusiasts. Did you know that there is more to the infamous Dr. Einstein than history dares to reveal? The world remembers him as the Father of Relativity, a visionary of physics, a pacifist—but what if I told you that wasn't the whole truth?

For instance, were you aware that Dr. Einstein worked for the U. S. Government from May 17, 1942 to June 30, 1946? He worked not only as consultant for the newly founded "Atomic Energy" program, but as the leading authority of an ultra "Top Secret" program that had to do with anti-radar devices. Dr. Einstein utilized his "Unified Field" theory while working on the latter's project.

From May 17, 1942 to June 30, 1946, Dr. Einstein was involved in probably **THE** most sensitive, and **THE** most bizarre government experiment ever carried out by our nation. This incident was so costly and failed so miserably, that to this day it remains classified under the highest designation—, **"TOP SECRET CODEWORD-MOST SENSITIVE"**

Yes, to this day the United States Government flatly denies, or for a better term, "ignores", the claim that this so-called "incident" ever occurred. They also insist that Dr. Einstein never worked for the government beyond a mere advisory role. Yet, the truth remains: some fifty crew members were either "destroyed" or simply "vanished," treated as nothing more than test subjects in a top-secret experiment beyond all imagination. And all the while, a humble, pacifist Dr. Einstein could only watch helplessly as an unprecedented event in history unfolded at the Philadelphia Naval shipyard between July 20 and August 20, 1943—the very disappearance of a US Navy warship, destroyer DL 173, the *USS ELDRIDGE!*

When it was all over, Einstein could only hang his head and somberly repeat over and over to himself, "What have I done? Those poor sailors! My God! I've killed them!"

His mind went back to Prussia and the words he so boldly spoke that fateful day:

Anything of unreality can be a reality…and what's more, these atoms, as well as other forces of nature, will give us the capability not only to win a battle, a war, or conquer a nation, but also to destroy all of mankind!

Just what was this ***PHILADELPHIA EXPERIMENT***? Stay tuned for Part Two of the series, entitled,
"CODEWORD – RIDERS UP"

Donovan let out a sharp laugh, shaking his head as he tossed the paper onto the table.

"Yea right!" he muttered.

He stood, stretching his arms overhead, shaking off the lingering unease from the article.

"Just like, 'Kirk, beam me up Scotty!'"

"'Aye, Captain! But we better hurry, lest the Klingons be gettin'ya first lad!'"

He smirked.

"What a bunch of crap! People will do anything for a story – especially guys like Cid! But then again, what an awesome novel this would make; a spy episode. Wonder if there's a book or movie about it? Clancy here I come!"

The phone rang. Donovan flinched. It was Cid. "Donovan, did you see the **YOU AND I** section this morning in the Herald?"

"Yea. Why?," Donovan asked in a slow monotone voice.

Cid shot back, eager to let the cat out of the bag, "Well, the guy writing that series is none other than Dr. Ronald Steinmetz's son!"

Donovan's stomach knotted.

His gaze drifted back to the article.

He exhaled, slow.

"I saw the name." His voice was flat, unreadable. "So it's him?"
"That's right!"

The silence between them continued for a moment, the weight of unspoken history setting in. Then Cid let out a humorless laugh, laced with something between bitterness and warning.

"My old boss! Don's pappy, the same one who sent me to Chile to get my ass shot up! Mr. Goddamn CIA himself!"

Donovan leaned forward, elbows on his knees, phone pressed tight against his ear. Then came the words that sent a chill through his spine.

"Something is going on, Mike."

CHAPTER TWO

I'M NOT A FAILURE

"Mr. Steinmetz, there is a call for you on line two. Are you busy?"

Don Steinmetz glanced up from his cluttered desk. His pulse picked up slightly—but he kept his voice even.

"No. I'll take it. Thanks, Marge."

Steinmetz was eager to find out who the first caller would be. He was also a bit skeptical. After all, he was the son of one of the former most powerful men in the United States. His heritage was full of government employees, except for him! He had somehow "failed". He had never gained recognition from his family for accomplishing anything that was not to their "approval". On the other hand, his older brother Mark was quite the "golden child", having been a premier athlete and scholar at West Point. After graduation, he was well on his way to following in his father's footsteps until he was killed in a helicopter accident in Panama in 1988. His father, the then Honorable Senator from Oklahoma went into mourning. He lost his re-election bid, then ended up in a senior care, mental institution, his mind spiraling into paranoia and trapped in conspiracy theories which only he believed.

And Don? Don had never been the heir his father wanted. He didn't go into politics. Didn't serve in the military. Instead, he became a journalist, chasing stories, hunting for truths no one wanted to hear. No one in his family ever acknowledged it. But they would. If this article blew up, they would.

Don's visits to his father were becoming more and more agonizing. Don tightened his grip on the steering wheel, his fingers white-knuckled as he pulled into the Hillsdale Senior Retirement Center parking lot. He had told himself this would be his last visit.

He couldn't stand to see his father gaze back at him as if he was a complete stranger. It was unbearable. But today marked the last visit Don would make to the Hillsdale Senior Retirement Center.

"Dad," he said, settling into the chair beside the old man's bed.

"I found some pictures of grand dad and you standing by the old Edsel. And I found some of Mark at West Point. Do you want them?"

The 76-year-old, grey-bearded senator looked into Don's eyes with a cold, dark stare and began, "Who are you? Why do you come here every week torturing me about my only son?"

Don's stomach clenched. Not today. Please, not today. But the old man's ranting spiraled.

"I lost him, you know! He's the last of our line. Who are YOU? What do you want? Money? Are you KGB? Please, my father didn't know anything. Call Colonel Kuznetsov. He will tell the truth, the *"Pravda"*. The Russians know more than we do about the energy source. You should know. You are KGB."

His father's voice rose, frantic, desperate, "Are you sending me away now? Who are you? Nurse! Nurse!"

The door burst open. A large woman of German descent ran into the room, her voice firm but kind, "Sir, you'll have to go!"

She met Don's gaze, her expression both apologetic and exhausted.

"Mr. Steinmetz, he doesn't know you anymore. He's getting worse. And each time you leave he becomes very depressed and very despondent. Then, he lashes out and starts rambling on about 'agents', 'termination', 'the other side', and 'secrets I can't tell'. After all this, he needs to be sedated for a week. So, Mr. Steinmetz, please try to understand…."

Don stared at his father. The old man was muttering to himself now, his mind lost in the secrets of a forgotten war.

Donald interrupted, "Yes, I do. It's been coming. He's too far gone. It's just that…" And with this, Don nodded at the stern-faced nurse who was now inserting an IV into the senator's arm. He turned and slipped out the door into the hallway, down the corridor, and out into the early sunset. His only thought was, "I have to get back to the paper. I have to finish"

Back at his desk, Don reached for his coffee, half-drained and cold, when the phone blared to life. Something about the urgency in the ring sent a prickle of unease down his spine. He hesitated for a second before he answered the phone.

"Hello! Hello!" a voice blared into Don's ear over the phone.

"Yes, this is Mr. Steinmetz. May I help you?" Don's heart began to beat faster and faster. His mouth began to quiver with anticipation.

The voice on the other end sent a soft, deliberate message, "LISTEN, YOU STUPID SON OF A BITCH! YOU ARE A FOOL. YOU ARE OPENING A DOOR TO A WORLD THAT YOU KNOW NOTHING ABOUT. ONE IN WHICH WILL CLOSE AND LOCK YOU AWAY FOREVER. STOP THE ARTICLE AND WE WILL LET YOU LIVE. DON'T, AND YOU WILL DIE. UNDERSTAND? LET IT GO! LEAVE US IN PEACE!"

Click. Dial tone.

Steinmetz went numb. He was scared to death. He looked around to see if anyone was watching him. He began to sweat. He hadn't expected anything like that! He thought he would receive a reaction of praise or constructive criticism; even a call from an "eyewitness". But not this!

For an instant, he thought maybe it was a prank. This wasn't just some angry reader with a grudge. This was real.

The fact of the matter was that he knew he'd attract attention but not in this fashion. At most, he figured some government agency would contact him and ask him where he got his information. But not a threat!

His first instinct was to pull the plug. To walk away. To tell himself this wasn't worth it.

But then—his journalist's instincts took over. And suddenly, the fear didn't matter.

He blurted out, "I GOT THIS!"

At 4pm Steinmetz sat down and began to write:

ATOM BOMB OR INVISIBILITY
SECOND OF A FOUR-PART SERIES
BY DON STEINMETZ
SPECIAL STAFF WRITER,
SAN DIEGO HERALD
CODEWORD – RIDERS UP

DECEMBER 20, 1941 – THIRTEEN
DAYS AFTER PEARL HARBOR
THE WHITE HOUSE

President Roosevelt sat in the briefing room, somber, his eyes affixed to the top secret message in front of him. Twelve of his top advisors sat in silence. You could read the President's mind and hear him think out loud.

Then, suddenly he snapped, "Gentlemen! We're in a Goddamn war!"

The room flinched. He leaned forward, glaring at each man in turn, his frustration coiling like a steel spring. "I was trying to buy time, but I knew the Japs were lying. There was no choice. I had to go with Europe and China on this one. We've been quietly trying to prepare things behind the scenes. But the bottom line is that you can't ask bi-planes to dogfight against fixed-winged Zeros, nor can you ask a soldier to use an M1 carbine against a 50 caliber machine gun! Those poor bastards never had a chance. Jesus! 2400 American lives! Why was I so naive? I should have ordered that AP on that lone PBY to shoot down that Zero they encountered. All those reports of a main battle group heading South and I...I just declared war on Japan a few days ago and now...well......We need to work fast boys!"

Nobody uttered a sound. You could see that President Roosevelt was profoundly hurt. You could sense the same rallying emotion that he had portrayed just a few days before in bringing the nation together and declaring war on Japan. He leaned forward, rested his huge arms on the table and slowly scanned the room staring into the eyes of each of the twelve high ranking officers and officials that were listening and paying strict attention to every word the President spoke.

Roosevelt broke the silence, "Admiral Hollins, henceforth, the Navy has a new department. It will be called THE OFFICE OF NAVAL RESEARCH. I want it manned within 72 hours with THE MOST capable and leading scientists this country has. Complete the staff with any personnel that fits your needs."

"Yes Mr. President", Hollins replied smartly.

Next, President Roosevelt turned to the others and ordered, "Now, everyone else go out and get me some horses....race horses! Anyone with a degree in physics, electricity, magnetism, hocus-pocus. Why, start with Einstein himself?"

A few mutters. A clearing of throats.

"Find out if there is some value to this INVISIBLE UNIFIED FIELD THEORY of his."

The air in the room grew noticeably heavier. "Gentlemen, this project is on a "need-to-know" basis only." His voice dropped.

"The classification is **TOP SECRET, CODEWORD – RACEHORSE.**"

He let the words settle. Then, without another glance, Roosevelt pushed back from the table. As he stood, everyone in the room shot up to attention. Without another word, he turned and strode out of the briefing room. The door clicked shut behind him.

After the President had departed from the briefing room, stares were exchanged and the silence continued for what seemed to be an eternity. All of them were trying to process the gravity of what had just been ordered.

Then, Admiral Hollins announced, "Gentlemen, you heard the President." A few curt nods. And without hesitation, each of the highest ranking members of the U.S. military and intelligence community quietly and subtly departed.

Yes, CODEWORD-RACEHORSE, began with the advent of the Office of Naval Research. Admiral Hollins wasted no time and assigned Rear Admiral Curtis Bensen to the organizational tasks. Bensen, in turn, enlisted Commander Hoxel, a man with a reputation for getting things done, no matter the moral gray areas. Their task? To build an elite scientific war council.

Within weeks, a hand-picked team of over forty naval officers, physicists, and engineers was assembled from across the country. Some were brilliant minds still reeling from the Great Depression, eager to be part of something bigger than themselves. Others were driven by sheer patriotism, determined to wield science as a weapon for the Allied war effort.

Some simply had no idea what they were truly signing up for. But they all had one thing in common—they were stepping into the unknown.

A place where science blurred into something far more dangerous. A place where the laws of physics were about to be rewritten.

After the majority of the group was assembled, Dr. Hoxel appointed one of the top civilian scientists, a Dr. Marvin Reno, to convince Dr. Einstein to once again take up his Unified Field Theory. Not an easy task, considering that Einstein had abandoned his Theory in 1927. He was afraid of its unknown and destructive power, and convinced it was going to bring an end to the world in the most violent way.

But here we see the first glimpse of something that I will reveal later – the making of a government cover-up. To this day although the US Navy refutes that Dr. Einstein worked for the government for any longer that a "a period of three months", an intriguing aspect can be found in the memoirs of his attorney, which reveal letters requested by family members, as to the research done by Einstein for the government from 1942-1946. A segment from the memoirs states:

"….as attorney for the Einstein estate, I sent, per family instructions, several requests to Washington requesting specific things that the Dr. had supposedly assisted in. I asked for both de-classified and non-classified information. Oddly enough, even after providing names, dates, as well as subject matter, I was denied any worthwhile material! The reply was that, "the good doctor did assist the office of Naval Research for a period of three months with some mathematical formulas for fueling devices, but other than this his services were limited." I decided to drop the matter due to some unexplained calls, visits, and death threats made to me and my family! On one occasion I received a letter from a retired Naval officer telling me to drop the inquiries because as he put it, "anyone trying to find out the truth about this, usually disappears." I dropped it. I told the family there was no further information."

These "racehorses" were assembled. Next, another code-word came down from Washington; **MORNING GLORY**.

This latest project was to have the group work on a device that would hide a navy ship from the enemy. Or, if you'll have it, to become "INVISIBLE"

For a year the committee developed theories, did endless experiments and performed endless calculations. Each member would have an assigned task and a due date. Then, all the members would gather and share data. Next, a device would be drawn up and tested. Nevertheless, time after time these projects were met with failure. Nevertheless, Dr. Reno was convinced that the Unified Field Theory of Invisibility was sorely needed at this point and was convinced that it would help end the war. He met with Einstein many times, seeking his participation. Finally, after much persuading, Einstein agreed. And, after several months they came up with a device that would indeed help "hide" a naval warship, or for the better to make it "disappear". And he did this by using electro-magnetic energy and combining it with gravitational fields using gigantic superconductors.

On May 17, 1942, Admiral Benson and Dr. Reno, sent by special courier, a 127 page highly classified document to President Roosevelt, entitled, **TOP SECRET, CODE-WORD 'MORNING GLORY',** or what would be known to become as, **"THE PHILADELPHIA EXPERIMENT".** An experiment that would make a ship disappear and transport it some two hundred miles away from its original location and make it reappear again off the coast of Virginia! But this episode would not only hide a ship, it would cause incredible havoc on many people and destroy the lives of all involved. More so, it would lead to the greatest government cover up aside from the Roswell incident of 1947.

In the early morning hours of July 16, 1943, at the Philadelphia Naval Shipyard,

the newly constructed, yet-to-be-commissioned destroyer, #DL-173-the USS ELDRIDGE, began to take on a dark green hue around its hull.

Naval officers stood at attention, their faces tense with anticipation as the lead scientist hovered over the controls. Every movement was deliberate, every order given with cautious precision. Then, with a deep breath, the switch was flipped.

A low noise vibrated across the air. The USS Eldridge was shaking. The dark green hue around its hull pulsed and intensified. And then—

It vanished.

The USS Eldridge disappeared for exactly five minutes. Then, as quickly as it had disappeared, it returned. From the deck of a nearby merchant vessel, stunned witnesses saw the ship fade back into view, materializing from the thick morning fog. But the horror wasn't over. Something was wrong. Horribly wrong. From the Eldridge, there were screams.

"I'm burning!"

"I'm on the other side!"

"My hands! My legs! They're gone!"

"God! Help me!"

The cries echoed across the bay, a haunting reminder that something had gone terribly, unspeakably wrong. And when the officers stepped onto the Eldridge, bodies were fused into the walls. Worse, some had disappeared completely.

Others were found still alive, but their minds had been broken beyond repair. The experiment had been a success, but at a terrible cost.

The horror aboard the USS Eldridge was too great to explain. It was silenced immediately. Files were sealed and survivors vanished.

And Albert Einstein, the man whose work had made it possible, would spend the rest of his life haunted by his own thoughts,

"What have I done?"

"Those poor sailors..."

"My God. I've killed them."

The United States Navy continues to deny that the Philadelphia Experiment ever took place. They claim Einstein never collaborated with them beyond an advisory capacity. They maintain that the Eldridge never vanished and that the Unified

Theory was never tested. However, the classified letters painted a different story.

As a matter of fact, a veteran naval officer once said, "Anyone trying to find out the truth about this experiment usually disappears."

Don, on the other hand, started to realize how accurate it was.

The article concluded with:

Next week: Part Three of the series, "SOMETHING WENT WRONG."

A closer look into the chilling aftermath of the Philadelphia Experiment. What truly happened to the USS Eldridge and its crew? Were they lost in time, trapped in another dimension, or sacrificed in a military experiment that had gone horribly wrong? The answers may be more terrifying than the questions. Stay tuned. The truth is closer than you think.

Don was still, calm and satisfied. He was lost in time and trapped in another dimension. His mind fought with the possibilities and the ridiculousness of it all but something about it seemed alarmingly believable.

Then he glanced at the digital clock on his desk. It was 1:30 am. He had been at it for twelve straight hours, consumed, driven—not just by work, but by something deeper. A relentless battle. A personal vendetta against life itself.

With a sigh, he switched off the computer, pulled on his sweater, and flipped off the light. As he walked out of the office, his voice broke the silence,

"I'm not a failure! I'm not a failure! I'm not a failure!"

The words stayed quietly in the empty hallway, but whether he was trying to persuade the world or himself, was another matter entirely.

CHAPTER THREE

HASTE MAKES WASTE

San Diego's streets were empty at this hour. Don Steinmetz pulled his coat tighter around him, his breath noticeable in the dim streetlights. The walk to the trolley station felt longer than usual, but that was just his nerves. He was on a high; his writing had been published, and the controversy had begun.

Despite that… He felt something in his gut—a hint of doubt. By this time tomorrow, every journalist in the country would be talking about him. He just needed to keep moving.

Steinmetz walked the eight blocks to the trolley station, and waited an hour for the 3am early Bird special. Then, he boarded the third car and took the first seat by the door. The cars were virtually empty. There was an old drunk in the first car and two sailors in the car that Steinmetz chose. The sailors were young. Both appeared to be in their early twenties. The first, was blond, standing about six feet or so, and thin. The second, was about five feet eight, heavy set with jet-black hair. Both had their Navy-issued pea coats over their wrinkled winter dress blues. Both appeared to be asleep after a night out on the town.

Don settled back in his seat, let out a deep breath, closed his eyes, and began to drift off. His mind drifted back to the article— the next piece in the series and the accolades he would receive, and

obviously, the controversy he would stir up. He thought, *"What the hell do I have to lose? I'll show these bastards! I'll be…"*
SCREEEEEECH.

The trolley suddenly came to a screeching, jolting stop, knocking Steinmetz to the floor of the car. The light went out, and a shrieking alarm resounded throughout the train.

Don was dazed from hitting his head on the rail of the seat in front of him. He was whiplashed then he was thrown forward and his head snapped back. He fell hard to the floor, trying to break his fall with his wrist and elbow. He was tossed around like a rag doll. As the train came to a stop, he found himself spread out on the deck underneath the seats and groping around in the dark for his glasses. Then, with a frightening and horrified sense of panic, he remembered his briefcase, *"Oh Christ! Where did it go?!"* Reaching out with his right hand, he began to flail helplessly and frantically, trying to find the black briefcase. His hands explored in the darkness, fingers brushing over the familiar ragged grip.

He managed to feel the recognizable frayed handle with his index finger. He tried to grab the handle and pull the briefcase towards him. As he did so, he felt a bit of relief as the briefcase's rectangular shadow now became somewhat clear.

He felt the presence of someone standing near him. As Steinmetz looked up he saw the unmistakable sailors' hats, and feeling comforted, he took a deep breath and remarked, "Thank God the Navy is here! You guys sure did take the right train!"

Just then, the emergency lights came on, and Steinmetz could now easily make out the faces of the sailors. The two sailors stood over him, their faces fully recognisable now.

There was something in both their looks that caused him to pause and suddenly become overwhelmed with sheer panic. Steinmetz's chest tightened and his pulse pounded in his ears as the taller blond bent down and snatched the briefcase from Don's hand, while whispering in his ear, "We sure **DID** take the right train asshole!"

Steinmetz froze. This wasn't random. This wasn't a mugging. Next, the dark-haired sailor leaned forward and looked Steinmetz coldly in the eyes and smirked.

Steinmetz's mind raced, then he began pleading, bargaining, scrambling for a way out. A confused fear overcame Steinmetz, "Who are you? What do you want? What is this? What…?"

In a plain, familiar, monotone voice, the same voice he had heard on the phone, the sailor replied, "I told you to let it die. You stupid son-of-a-bitch."

Next, Don saw the shiny point of a stiletto knife. His mouth contorted as he tried to explain, "No, please…it's just an article… fiction…it's….Do you want money?... I'll…"

With no hesitation and no wasted motion. The knife easily pierced through Steinmetz's skin and into his heart like a needle through cloth. Blood gushed everywhere. His mouth opened, but the only sound that came out was a wet, rattling gasp. Blood—so much blood—hot and thick, spilling down his shirt, pooling on the floor beneath him. His vision blurred.

A suffocating tightness gripped his lungs. His fingers twitched, reaching for something—anything. But there was nothing left to hold on to. The world darkened. The last thing he saw was the dark-haired man's smug, detached smirk. Then—Steinmetz collapsed.

His lifeless eyes stared at nothing.

Suddenly, the trolley lurched forward as if nothing had happened. A smooth, detached voice crackled over the PA system:

"Ladies and gentlemen, we apologize for that unforeseen event, but someone pulled the emergency stop lever. We'll be underway shortly. Thank you for your patience. We are sorry for any inconvenience that we may have caused you."

The two sailors stepped off the train at the 32nd Street Naval Shipyard exit, moving with calm and precision. They walked along the platform without rushing, their expressions unreadable. A sleek black limousine sped out of nowhere and came to a screeching halt. A side-door window opened halfway. The sailors approached the opened window. The blond sailor handed the briefcase to an outstretched hand protruding from the window. Neither man spoke. It was a silent transaction. Then, the front door swung open, but before either sailor could react, two muffled "pops" sounded. The sailors jerked once, twice, and then slumped on the pavement, their bodies spread out under the neon glow of a street lamp. Their blood poured into the asphalt cracks and merged with the shadows.

A voice from the rear seat of the limousine uttered, "Driver, Lindbergh Field please."

The driver nodded and replied, "Yes Mr. Senator!"

The limousine drove away, gliding into the night, leaving nothing behind but two bodies and a city that was asleep in unknown silence.

CHAPTER FOUR

URGENT

It was 7:45, on a Thursday morning, and the classroom was filled with subdued energy. The kids were restless, yet unusually polite and cooperative. Donovan stood in front of the class and leaned on his podium, "Ok man. Roll time, baby! No talking. Open your notebooks and do the warm-up on the board, please. Put the endings on the verbs."

A few groans and some lazy flipping of pages. "Comprenden? Bueno!"

The students chuckled and obediently began to do the work. They began to ask each other questions. Donovan didn't mind this type of talk because it was constructive. He went on taking roll and listening to his students,

"Jose, dude. What's the *"tu"* form of *"estar"* dude?

"Look in the *libro* dude!"

"Loser."

Donovan interrupted without haste, "No put-downs! Do your thing man!"

"Sorry D."

"No problema man."

Donovan was in the middle of re-teaching the aspects of the present tense of the Spanish verb *"estar"* when the door creaked open. David Hunter, Vice-Principal stepped inside. A stocky five feet ten-inch former power guard from Ohio State. It was too early for attendance or call slips, so this had to be serious.

Donovan locked eyes with him for a brief moment, then turned back to the class. He professionally finished his sentence and instinctively asked the students to open their texts to pages 230 and 231, then told them to silently study the charts for three minutes. Without missing a beat, he strode toward the door, where Hunter handed him a folded note. The word "URGENT" was scrawled across the top. Hunter leaned in, voice low, "If it's serious, I'll take your class and have Todd cover the rest of the day." Donovan nodded, already unfolding the paper. His winced as he began to read:

"Hi, I didn't want to disturb you, but call me ASAP!
There's been a murder – Steinmetz is dead. Someone
killed him on the trolley last night. And, his old man,
The Senator is MISSING! *- Cid"*

A cold wave rolled through Donovan's chest. He read it again. Questions poured through his mind; Steinmetz dead? The Senator is missing?

This was bigger than an article. Bigger than just a story. Hunter's voice snapped him back. "Donovan, do you need to go?" David asked.

Donovan nodded at Mr. Hunter and commented, "I just need to make a phone call."

He turned to his students, "Hey gang, I gotta make a phone call. Something's up with the boat. How about telling Mr. Hunter a story in Spanish?"

The students weren't really surprised and as usual, Bobby Jo broke the silence, "Sure Mr. D, what's her name? Did she fall outta the boat going to work this morning?"

Everyone laughed. Donovan smiled, "Behave. Be back in a sec."

He exited the classroom and made a mad dash across the patio area into the faculty lounge. He picked up the phone, dialed the customary "9" to get an outside line, and impatiently waited for the dial tone. He desperately punched in the numbers to the Daily Californian, *"574-4398"*.

Ring. Ring. Ring. Come on, Cid. Pick up.

More ringing. Then—A cheery voice: "Good morning. Daily Californian, may I…"

Donovan interrupted, "Cid Gilmore please."

"I'm sorry, that number is busy. Will you hold please?"

"No! Tell him it's Mike Donovan."

"But sir…"

"Please! It's life or death!"

After what felt like an hour, but was only a matter of a few short seconds, Cid's voice broke in, "Hey D. Guess you got my message. That was quick."

"Yea…What's up? Steinmetz?"

"Yeah, dead. And so are two sailors. Well, they weren't really sailors. They were…"

Gilman's voice stopped short, then continued, "Look man, let's do dinner. I have to get another story out. Besides, this sounds like there's more to it, and I don't want to talk on the phone."

Donovan understood. Both had held Top Secret Codeword, or TSC clearances. They were more than aware of security measures.

"Right on, man. Meet me at the Rusty Pelican at 1730."

"You got it. Oh yeah, what did your kids say about the note?

"You know, the usual – boat, girl…"

"1730".

Donovan hung up the phone and exhaled. He became anxious but maintained his poise.

Donovan raced back to his class, forcing himself to relax, then slipped into teacher mode as soon as he reentered the class. As he did so the students were laughing hysterically. Mr. Hunter was showing the class an old baseball card. Not just any card - a TOPS card of Donovan in his K. C. Royals uniform. It was his rookie picture taken on the first day of spring training at the age of 18, fresh off the Helix High School baseball field.

The kids stopped and became silent. Then Mr. Hunter commented, "We need to put this in the Year Book, Mr. Donovan."

The kids burst out laughing again.

"Ok, ok. Thank you, Mr. Hunter," Donovan said with a smirk. One of the girls blurted out, "Hey, Mr. D, nice pants."

Joey added, "D, did you know I have your card? It's up to 33 cents!"

The class broke out in a chorus of laughter again. Donovan laughed along with the jokes as Hunter smiled and slipped out of the room unnoticed.

"Ok," Donovan started, "Repita, *como, comes, come, comemos, comen.*"

The entire class erupted in a crescendo, *"COMO, COMES, COME….!!!!"*

The last class had finished repeating the verbs. Donovan's voice had become a bit hoarse, and before he could say, "Have a nice day," the 2:30 bell rang and the *"adios"* was given.

Mike didn't stop to check his mailbox for fear of being detained in any conversations. He went directly from his class to Mast Boulevard, walked over the bridge, and ran up the stairs to his apartment.

It was 2:45. The apartment was silent, except for the faint blinking of the answering machine's red light. He hit the play button. A woman's calm, professional voice filled the room: "Mr. Donovan, this is the San Carlos Library. " Your books are in; *The Philadelphia Experiment*, by Charles Berlitz and Ray Moore, and, *What Einstein Really Knew*, by Kaite Sherrod."

A brief pause. Then, something shifted in the tone of her voice and continued, "But the other book you requested, entitled *Fifteen Missing Men*, by Howard Henkle, has been classified as *missing*."

Donovan became frustrated, "Classified? Library books didn't just vanish—not like this. This wasn't an overdue return. Someone had made it disappear."

"Please come in as soon as you can. We'll hold these for one week."

BEEP. The message ended.

Mike stood frozen, staring at the machine. His mind raced. There was no time to think. He grabbed his keys and was out the door in seconds, practically vaulting down the stairs, his heartbeat pounding louder than his footsteps. Something wasn't right.

He jumped in his blue Ford XLT and after struggling to find the right key, inserted it into the ignition, started up, threw the transmission into drive and sped off to the San Carlos Library.

CHAPTER FIVE

THE REUNION

The parking lot at the Rusty Pelican Restaurant on Harbor Island was empty as Donovan pulled in. He parked his truck in the first stall facing San Diego Bay. It was 5:30 pm on the dot. Cid was usually thirty minutes late, so he began to skim through the pages of his newly acquired "Research". Donovan reached for the stack of books on the passenger seat, pulled out <u>The Philadelphia Experiment</u> by Charles Berlitz, and hastily began to read. What started as idle skimming the pages, turned into full immersion. He devoured the introduction, then dove into the first two chapters.

His reading began with the likes of two Air Force cadets talking to a former naval officer about a bizarre experience that the latter had encountered. As he read on, he came across words such as; *metallic, organic invisibility, the flames, and of course, The Unified Theory.* Names such as Einstein, Allende, Brown, and Jessup further piqued his attention, pulling him deeper into the mystery.

Reality slid just a little as his imagination took over. He sat back in his seat, the lines playing out in his mind as vivid thoughts, as if he were watching a movie - and HE was in it!

Donovan began to drift off, murmuring under his breath, *"Ladies and gentlemen. I am proud to introduce to you the man that has solved the greatest military and government cover-up of the modern era….Mr…"*

"Hey, honky! Wake up! And don't forget to put me someplace in the book, ok?" The abrupt voice startled Donovan out of his daydream. He looked up at the familiar person, grinning as he recognized the one person who could call him that and still live. Donovan smirked. "Hell bro, you're gonna be the main man!"

Cid chuckled and slid into the seat across from him. "What the hell are you reading, teach?" Cid asked.

Donovan held up the book. "Books, like the *Philadelphia Experiment* and *What Einstein Really Knew.*"

Cid continued, "Well teach, if what I think is going on, you gonna need more than Philadelphia and Einstein to help." Cid stopped short and started to shake his head as the weight of their past hovered between them, "Ah, shit man. We can't be diving back into this jive-ass scrap no more. You're a teacher now. You ain't no *spook* no more. And I'm an editor, not no-*terminator*! It ain't '78. It ain't Iran, helos, terrorists, black boxes, KGB, MI-6, CIA, bombs…"

Donovan's eyes met Cid's. They stared at each other in disbelief. Then they both burst out laughing. High fives were exchanged. Cid yelled, "Bombs or bullshit! Once a spook…"

Donovan finished the familiar naval saying, "…always a spook!"

Cid leaned back and threw his hands up. "Let's eat, teach!" Cid suddenly blurted. "Then, let's take ole USS NEVERDOCK for a ride. Whaddya say?"

Donovan, still laughing, replied, "Sure. But did you know that when you get fired up, your ebonics go off the charts!"

After a few glasses of Merlot, salad, oysters, and more Merlot, they exited the Rusty Pelican and made their way down to the docks. As they strolled toward the docks under the velvet San Diego sky, their conversation danced between old memories from the newsroom, past missions, and the wild stories of students who'd left lasting impressions in their classrooms. Time hadn't dulled their bond—it had only made the stories better. It was unusually warm and clear for a February evening, as Mike and Cid boarded the forty-foot Pacemaker pleasure craft which was located at the Cortez Marina. Donovan started the twin 22-horsepower Crusader engines, untied the dock lines, and skillfully backed the *Pelican Watch* out of its slip. The engines purred as Mike put the levers in the forward position. "All ahead dead slow!" Cid ordered. "Aye aye skipper!" Donovan shot back, pushing the levers gently forward.

The water was still and smooth like a mill pond, as the motor yacht made its way past the endless rows of docks and berthing. Then, the duo headed out into the serene waters of San Diego Bay.

The two stood on the flybridge as the engines' *RPMs* increased and the speedometer climbed to 10 knots. They cruised past the aircraft carriers, the USS KITTY HAWK and the USS NIMITZ. As they did, the massive warships dwarfed the tiny pleasure craft. Both men fell silent partly from melancholy and partly from respect. The presence of the carriers—reminders of wars past and missions classified—said enough. They steered away and aimed toward the twinkling lights of Seaport Village, where the skyline shimmered in the reflection of the bay. The reflection on the water revealed the old BERKLEY and THE STAR OF INDIA as they passed Broadway Pier. After they had taken the usual tourist route, Cid, taking on the bark of an admiral, ordered, "Right full rudder, all ahead full! Set a course for the Coronado Bridge. Come to a heading of 160 degrees." And with that, Donovan grasped both throttle levers and slammed them all the way forward. The Pacemaker lurched ahead and the bow came out of the water. The gauges registered 2800 *RPMs* each, and the speed indicator now read 30 knots. "Aye, admiral!" Donovan responded, the thrill of the ride taking hold.

Within five minutes, the Pelican Watch came to rest under the Coronado Bridge. Donovan shut the engines down, walked up to the bow, undid a line, and dropped the anchor into the bay. After a few moments, he felt the slack and knew the anchor had hit bottom. He let out a little more line, checked the drift, then tied the remaining line to the cleat on the bow of the boat.

Donovan turned off the engines when the Pelican Watch had settled into a leisurely drift beneath the Coronado Bridge. The night had fallen completely—calm, crisp, and silent. Donovan broke out two captain's chairs from below decks and brought them out on the fantail. It was close to 10:30 pm by now. A soft crescent moon was suspended above San Diego, casting a dim light over its two million citizens. There were no other boats in sight and the only thing that could be heard was the rhythmic clanging of buoy number 1A that guided all naval vessels safely under the bridge and to their berths at the 32nd Street Naval Station.

"It doesn't get any better than this, Mikey!" Cid exclaimed.

Donovan nodded in agreement and began, "Yea, out here you can be anyone you want to be: a sailor, a teacher, a ballplayer, a …"

"A writer?" Cid asked in a matter-of-fact entrapping tone.

Donovan hesitated, then smirke, "Yea, why?"

"Well, you've always wanted to be another Tolstoy or Chekhov." Cid said with a sly smile, swirling the last sip of Merlot in his glass. "Here's your chance!"

Donovan became leery, yet his curiosity prevailed. He set his glass down slowly. "What the hell do you mean? You've brought me out here to tell me more than just about Steinmetz's death. So out with it!"

Cid didn't respond right away. Instead, he stood up and walked to the railing, placing both hands on the cool metal as he stared out across the bay. The city lights shimmered in his dark eyes. For a moment, all was quiet except for the soft lapping of water against the hull. Then he turned to Donovan, his expression serious. "Look," he said, voice low, "They wouldn't expect you."

Donovan's voice rose in anger, "What do you mean by '*they*'?"

Cid sighed and ran a hand down his face. "Well, the series about the hocus-pocus shit man. I mean, well, there's got to be more to it. Maybe Steinmetz WAS on to something big." He paused, locking eyes with Donovan. "It's up to me, uh, us, to find out what."

Donovan leaped to his feet and shouted, "You mean you want ME to be the next trolley stain?" he snapped. "No thanks!"

"Goddamn it, Donovan!" Cid's voice boomed, frustration slipping through his usual cool demeanor. Donovan held up a hand. "Cid, just tell me what you know about Steinmetz. Then I'LL THINK about it."

A long silence passed between them, the tension hanging thick in the salty air. Then Cid, the fire in his eyes cooling, retorted sarcastically, "That's the spirit, teach!" he said, sinking back into his seat with a grin. "Now, how about a wine cooler?"

Donovan went below to the galley, got two berry wine coolers and brought them topside. The clink of the glass bottles echoed softly across the bay as he stepped onto the deck. Cid had pulled the other captain's chair close to Donovan's, anticipating a lengthy talk.

Donovan unscrewed the tops and handed one of the coolers to Cid who sat back, took a sip, tilted his head back, and then began in a very determined tone, "Don Steinmetz. He was a loser as a kid. I went to school with him at UCSD. I learned a great deal about him from many different sources. Seems his old man, my boss, left enough money for his first son Bobby, an athletic and bright young man, who was pegged to be President of the United States someday." Cid took another sip, his jaw tightening.

"Don, on the other hand, was a rebel who did everything NOT to please his old man." He gave a faint shake of his head as if still trying to make sense of it. "Oh, he tried, but he just couldn't quite *get it* all the time." Cid paused, watching the reflection of the city lights ripple in the water.

"He hated school," he said plainly. "Barely graduated from high school. He did like to write and when he decided to go into journalism he had to start at a community college, get an AA degree, then transfer to a no-name college."

Donovan nodded slowly, listening. No interruptions. He knew better than to break Cid's rhythm. "His dad helped him get into UCSD," Cid continued. "And when he did finally "graduate", he felt sorry for him, so he got him a job at the Herald. Not out of pride but out of pity." Cid leaned back in the chair with a quiet sigh, gently cradling the wine cooler in the palm of his hand and continued,

"Bobby, though? Bobby got everything. The Senator poured every dime into his education and athletic desires. He went on to West Point, graduated in the top ten, and went off to fly helos." He stopped, his expression tightening.

"Then Bobby gets killed. Chopper crash. The night before he was supposed to deploy to Europe. That crushed the old man. He lost his re-election bid, left his wife of fifty years, and went into seclusion. Next thing you know, he's in a whacko house, sedated to the max. To top this off, he has a 24-hour bodyguard."

Donovan gave a deep frown, "Guarded?"

Cid gave him a look. "Yup!"

He took another sip before continuing, more bitterly now,

"Meanwhile, Don's career took off slowly at the Herald but eventually he made a name for himself. Scraping for attention. Nevertheless, his father never acknowledged him for any success. No approval. Not one damn word. It drove Steinmetz crazy with jealousy and resentment." He exhaled hard, the frustration showing in his tone and on his face.

"He became depressed, and except for his writing, he was pretty much a recluse. Trying to always 'please' his father and gain 'acceptance', he was always researching weird hype like UFOs and the HANGER 51 crap. But the biggest thing is that he never reached what we call, 'editorial ego.'" He paused again, then leaned forward.

Cid swirled the last of his wine cooler in the bottle, his voice dropping to a quieter, more controlling tone,

"He just didn't have it." He leaned back, sighing. "Now, here is where it gets even more strange." Donovan sat forward, sensing the shift.

"See, Don got a hold of some of his father's old letters. Personal stuff. And in them, he found references to a top-secret government project from the 1940s—something deep, buried. His dad wasn't just a senator, Mike. He chaired a committee that handled the budgets for... 'Sensitive Projects.

"Turns out, one of those projects involved radar development. Don's old man refused to sign off on funding. Said it was unstable or unethical—who knows? But that pissed off a lot of powerful people. He lost a chunk of political capital overnight."

Cid paused, and looked Donovan right in the eyes and said, "The irony is that it was right after this decision not to support the project, that Bobby died." The silence lingered.

"A few years went by. Then, one day, Don decided that he was going to light the world on fire. He started writing his '*Series*'." Cid shook his head slowly.

"Well, Don, maybe he knew it would stir the hornet's nest. Maybe that was the point. But what he *didn't* count on... was how fast they'd come for him. And they did. Now he's dead. So are those two phony sailors. The Senator? Gone. Vanished. Like he never existed."

Cid trailed off. Suddenly, Cid's voice was halted by Donovan, who had been listening intently to every word. "Only now" he said, mimicking Cid's voice. "Only now, here's where I come in to write the third and FINAL part. They'll come after me, we'll go after them."He stood now, pacing the deck.

"Then, we'll prove that a ship did disappear and that guys went ape shit, vanished, and 'got stuck'. We'll also, in the meantime, find the clues to Morris Jessup's death, the whereabouts of 15 sailors, ten prominent scientists, and three naval officers that nobody has heard from since 1943. And, to top it all off, we'll prove that there WAS a government cover-up; a cover-up that is directly responsible for not only the Philadelphia Experiment, the Roswell incident, and the Hanger 51 bullshit, not to mention, some newfound 'power' source based on Einstein's Unified Field Theory." Donovan hung his head and gave a deep sigh.

"After all this, if I'm still alive, I'll be famous! CHRIST ALL MIGHTY CID!"

Cid Gilmore stared at Donovan with a look of satisfaction. Then, in a burst of disbelief, he shot up from his chair, nearly knocking over his wine cooler.

"That's right you son-of-a-bitch!" he shouted, pointing a finger. "But how did you know all of this shit? Jesus Rodriquez Chuckee Cheeses coach!"

Donovan smiled at Gilmore and simply remarked, "You're always late, so I had a chance to read my library books!"

Cid returned to his thoughts and continued, "Ok, what we have is a note they found in Steinmetz's coat pocket. It reads, *"Wouldn't they like to know the truth? Well, I have it!" Things to do:*

1. *Contact archives,*
2. *Kuznetsov, he had the book, <u>Fifteen Missing Men</u>,*
3. *3rd in a series due by 9 am next Wednesday.*

He paused. "That's it. No other clues. Nothing else." He turned to Donovan, eyes sharp.

"That's it. No more clues. Nothing. Look, Donovan, it's still there, and you know it! That desire to get that last submarine, find out where that last classified info is! We could sell this story and make a killing.

"Or it could kill us!" Donovan shot back.

Cid gave a half-smile, the kind born of knowing too much and living through worse. Cid continued, "Besides, maybe the

Philadelphia Experiment DID take place. Maybe Einstein WAS right. Maybe man can control every molecule. Perhaps there is something to this molecular reorganization."

Donovan stopped Cid and asked, "Where do we start?"

Cid smiled a big wide smile and replied, "RUSSIA! Mr Kuznetsov himself, my man. My main man and Mr. Double KGB himself. I'll get the book for you, and you do the rest!"

"Who was this Kuznetsov, Cid?"

"He happens to be one of the first Soviet Spies to have worked on invisibility projects on both sides of the fence. He gave me info, and I gave him info."

"But why would YOU need info on projects like that?" Donovan asked with surprise.

"Because teach, I worked for the old man. Remember? We had to find out if it would have been worth funding our own projects!"

"Cid, you bastard! You never told me!"

"Well, honky man. It's late. And you have to teach tomorrow."

Donovan didn't say a word. He went to the bow, pulled up the anchor, then returned to the helm. He started the engines and began a slow, silent cruise back to the marina, all the while thinking to himself, *well, 3 and 2 bases loaded, bottom of the ninth. Donovan swings! That ball is going, going…"*

Cid bid farewell, made his way to the parking lot, hopped in his sports car, and sped off. After a thirty-minute drive, he arrived at his secluded luxurious condo in Rancho Bernardo. Once inside, he clicked on his computer, punched in the email address to the Russian Embassy, and waited for the prompt. The "contact us" heading came up, and Cid entered a five-group numerical code called a *flazhnyij*. After a few seconds, another prompt came up with the title,

"Enter acceptance number". He punched in four sets of five number groups and waited. A few minutes later, an email popped up with the name "Chajka", Kuznetzov's username. Next to it was the introduction, "Welcome to the Russian Federation. How may I assist you?"

Cid then typed the following message, "dyada moroz". Immediately, the response came back, "Go to secure comms". With this, Cid pulled out a red cellphone from his briefcase, turned it on, and when he heard the dial tone, he entered four more groups of five-digit numbers then hung up.

The phone rang back. On the other end, a voice resounded, "Koshka how are you?"

With a smile on his face and a sigh of relief, Cid responded to the familiar voice, "I'm good Medved. How are you?"

"Nu, khorosho….kak mozhno pomogat' tebe?"

"Well, I need - "THE BOOK!""

"Ok, Kuznetzov replied willingly "Da konechno. My research has been updated, and I have included it in the margins and in the back. Most importantly, I have found out what happened to the 15 missing sailors. They were committed to VA hospitals across the United States. Eight have died from natural causes, five have committed suicide, one is in the late stages of dementia, and the last one escaped from his hospital and is living in the mountains in Colorado. He is 80 and of sound mind. We contact him once a month. I will send the book to you via our mail. You can pick it up at the consulate in San Francisco in two weeks. Meantime, I will get in touch with "MAX", that's his codename. He is about 50 miles from Denver living on an abandoned cattle ranch."

"Ok, *spasibo bol'shoe*"

"You are welcome, my old friend. I read the newspapers too and have been receiving your messages as to what has been going on. Donovan is a good choice to take over for Steinmetz. What a fool Steinmetz was. I will let MAX know you will be contacting him and will make arrangements. Poka."

"Wait, *podozhdi*...who was the last man? The one that you talk to once a month?"

"He was actually a witness. His name is ALENDE!"

"Oh my God! THE Alex Alende that gives talks at science fiction lectures?"

"*DA*. But his son was one of the sailors that died in the hospital."

"I see...*poka*...Later Medved."

"Koshka out."

The line went dead exactly three minutes after the call started to avoid any chance of tracing the call.

The phone rang. It was Donovan. "Hey Cid, what archives do you think Steinmetz was thinking about?"

"Ours of course. And you know that book you said was lost? Well, you were half right. To people here, it IS lost, but to my Russian contact it has been "found"; it is the Russian Embassy in Washington DC. It was stolen by a tourist."

"This tourist, is he a friend of yours?"

"Why....I should say not."

CHAPTER SIX

RIDERS IN THE SKY

"PAPA, ALPHA, KILO, I authenticate: ROMEO, NOVEMBER, MIKE, DELTA. How copy? Over."

The C-130 pilot repeated the *secure comm* call with Lancaster Marine Base, located roughly forty miles southwest of San Angelo, Texas. Lancaster sat in the middle of a wasteland. It was a *non-existent* base that was used to test high tech weapons on the newest fighter aircraft. As customary, any classified military flight passing through the airspace would check in with Lancaster control.

Marine Staff Sergeant Malcom Essex was monitoring the C-130's progress. After the initial call-up, Malcom broke his own silence, "Roger, X-RAY, ZULU, BRAVO. I authenticate: ROMEO, NOVEMBER, MIKE, DELTA. How copy? Over."

Lt Commander Danielle Collin's voice came crackling through her throat mic, "Roger ZULU, CORAL 3O for 234. I have PAPA. How copy? Over."

Essex, the ever-disciplined Marine, answered back, "Roger KILO. You have PAPA."

Instinctively, as Collins climbed to 35,000 feet and increased speed to just over 280 knots her eyes scanned the instrument panel. She caught sight of an unidentified radar blip that was not responding to IFF. It was some 100 kilometers out, and she thought it strange that Essex hadn't picked up on it. She radioed

Lancaster again, "ZULU, this is KILO. What do you hold at 301 at 90 clicks? Over?"

Essex came back with what seemed odd to Collins, as if it was some "prepared response", "KILO, I show no BOGIES, no INDIOS. Over?"

Just as the ten-year top-notch naval pilot realized something was amiss, a horrible burst of static blasted through her headsets. She ripped them off and threw them to the deck, swearing out loud, "Old shit never works!"

She kept following the blip with intensity, and she became increasingly concerned as the "BOGIE" was only some 50 kilometers to the northeast. "Now, who the hell is this? Santa?"

She turned to her co-pilot, Lt Russ Wilkins, a four-year Lt. Jg, fresh out of the Naval Academy who was just regaining consciousness from a deep sleep and slowly sitting up to scan the horizon.

"Russ, what the hell do you make of that BOGIE at 302 at 45? I mean, Lancaster can't confirm it, and it has no ID. Just registers a speed of 400 knots plus!"

Russ, the ever-sarcastic helper, replied, "Well mam, maybe it's one of those *sightings*. I mean, we ARE flying over the desert in restricted airspace."

Christ, Russ, do you always have to be such a smart ass? I mean, there's no truth to any of that crap, and you know......OH SHIT! WHAT THE HELL...."

The Lt. Commander's voice trembled as both felt a "thud" just under the belly of the aircraft. The C-130 started to shudder and lose altitude. A loud, high-pitched whistle sounded in the cockpit, indicating that they had been hit. Then, the roar of what seemed to be a million-horsepower engine could be felt passing right over the top of them. "JESUS RUSS! WHAT THE FUCK! WHAT THE HELL WAS THAT? WE'RE GOING DOWN. GRAB THE YOKE AND HELP ME!"

Russ was already reaching for the yoke and the throttles, applying full power. He increased the flaps by 20 percent and tried to right the struggling aircraft.

"I think we just got overflown by that BOGIE. That was a jet wash. What the…"

Collins' attention turned to their "cargo," and she asked Russ to check on it, "Go see how our passenger is doing"

Russ blurted through the PA system, "Senator, this is the co-pilot. Hang on sir. We've run into some turbulence." Russ' voice stopped sooner than it had begun. A deep, calm voice could be heard through the open mic, "I'm fine so far. Now get me the hell out of here and on the ground. Are we almost in Mexico?"

Then, a flash of light and a ball of fire enveloped the plane. Collins and Wilkins had time for one last desperate glance at each other before there was silence.

Back at Lancaster, Sergeant Essex turned his eyes away from the radar screen, straightened, and affixed them smartly on the gentleman standing over his shoulder. Then reported, "General, sir, PAPA has been terminated."

Three-star General Fitz Hobson nodded his approval to Essex and replied, "Very well, Sergeant. Contact RANGER and send him home."

"Yes sir, RANGER ONE, this is CHARLIE BRAVO. Return to FOXTROT."

The voice on the other end came back with a stutter of broken English and a heavy Russian accent. "Da, CHARLIE BRAVO, for to be mission complete. Return now."

The Russian pilot turned to his co-pilot and ordered, "Na bazu. Dovernu na kurs 350."

The unmarked Russian stealth MIG 36A descended to treetop level and headed for the Gulf of Mexico and the Russian aircraft carrier, the VOLKOV.

As soon as the termination was completed, General Hobson turned and nodded to two plain- clothes men that were with him.

They drew two 9mm pistols with silencers aimed at Essex and another operator and shot them dead. Hobson and the two men exited the control spaces. As they did, Hobson lobbed a grenade into the room to make sure no evidence was left behind. After the explosion, the three men boarded an unmarked black jeep and sped off toward the open desert.

CHAPTER SEVEN

LIFE GOES ON

SANTEE, CA
THURSDAY NOVEMBER 26

"Claire, I'm going to see Mrs. Bruner, herself, Madame Editor in Chief of THE HERALD, the award-winning newspaper of San Diego. Please tell people I went to play hoops for lunch."

Soft spoken, good-natured Claire nodded as Cid flew out of the front door and hopped in his red Miata that was parked in a space marked, "EDITOR ONLY." He pulled out of the lot and onto Second Street, then finally onto Highway 8, heading west to Mission Valley and the San Diego Herald's main offices. As he leaned back and settled into his plush black vinyl seats, he tuned the radio to KSDO 1130 News just in time to catch the sports.

"…so the Chargers have a big task ahead of them this year, Humphry's having some shoulder problems, the defensive line losing two veterans in one week. We'll see how the rookies step up to the show. In horse racing, it was Wild N' Nice winning the Hollywood feature over the weekend…"

This caught Cid's attention immediately. All the code words in the series by Steinmetz had to do with horseracing. He thought aloud, *"Damn, I've got to convince the old lady to continue the story.*

She likes those horses. That's what I'll do. I'll get her some tips from that jockey at Del Mar whom I know. Jeff Houser. If she'll continue the series, I'll have the foot in the door that we need. Donovan, the author. Ah, what a joke! I need a Russian linguist, a guy who knows what the Russian pilots are saying. But Christ! He's a friend. Teamwork baby!"

"Well, you see, Mrs. Bruner, Don and I were long-time friends. His father was the source of most of the information he was gathering—everyone in the family knew.

It's no secret, So, I have the rest of Don's material and his research papers. You see, he made it a point to make a copy of everything and give them to me just in case anything happened to him...You understand. So I'd like permission to continue the series, using this material and employ a ghostwriter of sorts, someone that is current on these matters, yet will remain obscure to the public. I have just the person..."

With that Mrs. Bruner. The fiery-eyed seventy-year- old self-taught, self-made editor-in-chief, leaned back in her hunter-green leather chair and put her hands in her lap. She sighed, looked out the window, and then interrupted Cid with a barrage of defensive statements, "Look, I'm not going to continue the series, Mr. Gilmore. I'll not risk it. Besides, Don is dead, his own father is dead or missing, and that in itself makes it too frightening! Now if you will, please excuse me."

Cid really knew what the old lady would say. She always denied requests at first, *"have to talk to the attorneys"*, that's what's on the old lady's mind. He had seen it time after time with her and her empire; do nothing unless it benefits her and her paper without the slightest chance of liability. But, within the hour, she will call back and say "yes". She isn't going to turn this down. She

KNOWS there are too many other press sources waiting in line for this one, especially *THE DAILY CALIFORNIAN*!

Before Cid thanked Mrs. Bruner for her time, he mentioned he could get some racing tips from a jockey friend at Del Mar and a personal interview on the inside workings of the track. Solemnly, he excused himself.

Upon arriving back in his office in El Cajon, Claire had already left a handwritten message on his desk marked *"URGENT."*

Cid dialed the Herald's number and told the receptionist who it was, and she immediately transferred his call. Mrs. Bruner's voice boomed through the speaker, "Mr. Gilmore, I do apologize. After careful consideration, we will continue the series for the benefit of our readers. Would you still be interested in assisting us? And how about those racing tips?"

Cid was holding his hand to his mouth and grinning. It was all he could do to keep from laughing out loud, "Why, Mrs. Bruner, thank you. I'll get on it right away. I suggest we explain to the readers just what we're doing or give them SOME reason. Let me take care of that." Bruner asked, "But who will be doing the writing?"

Cid smiled as he couldn't wait to arouse Bruner's curiosity, "Oh, a person we'll call James Davis. Trust me."

"Ok, Mr. Gilmore."

Cid couldn't wait to call Donovan. He was lucky when he got a hold of him on the second ring. "Hello, " Donovan answered.

"D! What up? Listen, get ready. I need a lead to the final series. You know that guy in the book that you started telling me about? Well, here is what we have to do."

Donovan interrupted, "Wait!" Why don't YOU write the lead?" "Look, style man! Style. You can imitate it better than anyone. But nobody's going to expect you, remember? Now take some notes and get ready to, well, maybe be the next *Chekov*?"

Donovan grabbed a pen and a yellow pad of paper. *"Ok boss, I'm ready boss."*

CHAPTER EIGHT

THE HORSES ARE IN THE GATES

Donovan had written as fast as Gilmore had dictated. He was trained to do so. As a Russian linguist, you had to be able to copy "*flazhnyj*" group numbers that related to shipping as fast as they came over the radio. Yes, the hand IS quicker than the eye – quicker than even the ear, for that matter. Donovan remembered when he could listen to Soviet fighter activity with both ears.

"Christ," he muttered to himself, "I could keep up with vectored SU-15s in one ear and a missile shot from a TU-95 in the other ear at the same time! I was good." A smirk crept across his face.

He continued, "And not to mention chasing Soviet nuclear subs all over the Mediterranean Sea…yes, I was DAMN good!"

Donovan began to write out his notes and then organized them. This was his big chance—well, even if he did have to use a pseudonym!

Cid knew exactly what he was doing when he picked the name James Davis. It was a calculated move, meant to keep whoever was behind all this interested. You see, James Davis was one of two Air Force cadets (the other being Ronald Aimes) who were indirectly, but importantly involved historically with all of this. Using this name would, hopefully, Cid and Mike thought, would bring out the two from hiding if they were still around.

You see, back in 1970, there was an unusual encounter on a clear summer's night at the Air Force Academy in Colorado Springs, Colorado.

A short, strange-looking bald man of about eighty approached Davis and asked him how he liked the Air Force. Davis told him he liked it, then asked the man who he was. The gentleman didn't reply. Instead, he just started rambling on about his past, his voice low and distant. "I was in the service", he began, tilting his head toward the sky as if searching for some object in deep space. He looked into Davis's eyes with a black stare.

"I was a Naval officer during WWII. The Navy did things to me. They made me nuts! Then, they denied everything and sent me out to pasture! Bastards! They hurt a lot of good people!" He leaned in closer, his voice trembling. "They fried people up! They made us disappear, you know. Some of us made it back. We were the lucky ones. There were fifteen of us. But the rest of the crew didn't make it back."

His eyes flickered, haunted. "They got left on the other side. They, kind of, well…..*froze*. Some guys vanished right in mid-air, while still others *melted* into the bulkheads."

He paused, swallowing hard. "There were a couple of guys that fell from nowhere onto the deck screaming, *"Send me back!"*, *"Help me! Where am I?"*.

He shook his head slowly. "It was pretty horrible to watch. To hear."

A long silence stretched between them before he continued, softer this time.

"Me? I felt like I was freezing to death. At one point I found myself floating in the air looking down. To my astonishment, the ENTIRE ship was floating in the air with me." He looked Davis dead in the eye.

"It was a destroyer you see, the ELDRIDGE. Some type of classified bullshit they were doing. We were all volunteers."

Then, almost in a whisper, he added: "Einstein was there too. Well..."

Davis started to feel a bit anxious and blurted out, "Well sir, I'm sorry that happened. I have to get back now."

But the old guy started to flail his arms in the air and began to cry. "Well, they told me my name was Humes, Allen Humes, LTJG. But I knew my name. I just... forgot it for a while."
He clutched at the air, desperate now. "But... a merchant marine fellow by the name of Carl Allende told me who I really was. He said he saw the whole thing from his ship, said he'd been trying to track us down, and even gave lectures on the incident."

Davis froze. The man's eyes were wide and trembling, his voice now a frantic whisper.

"I do know there was an Electrician Mate Second Class and he was installing these huge generators on board the Eldridge and...."

His words trailed off into something unintelligible, lost somewhere between memory and madness. Our dear little fellow suddenly fell silent. His look became perplexed and depressed "I'm sorry, son," he said softly. "You don't need to hear any of this"

"No, it's okay sir. Well, you take care." Davis replied, then hesitated. "But I need to ask you. Why are you here?

Without hesitation, Humes shot back, his eyes now burning with purpose, "To tell the truth son. To tell the truth."

Donovan cracked a smile as he reread his notes and remembered what he had once read in the *Philadelphia Experiment*, by Charles Berlitz. He began to write down what Cid had dictated. Then after the first few words, he stopped, sighed, and exclaimed, "*Screw this.*" he muttered. "*I know this. I'll write the series – my way!*"

CHAPTER NINE

THIRD AND FINAL IN A SERIES

ATOM BOMB OR INVISIBILITY
FINAL PART
BY JAMES DAVIS, VOLUNTEER STAFF WRITER
SAN DIEGO HAROLD

Dear readers,

My name is James Davis. I am a volunteer scientific writer for the Herald. I will attempt to piece together the remaining notes of the late talented Mr. Steinmetz's research so that I may complete the series and satisfy YOU, the reader.

The Herald's small lead-in led to the mention of an archeology and physics professor at Stanford University, Dr. Thomas Reinhardt, a scientist and lecturer. A robust man even at seventy-five, he still had a full set of dark brown curly hair.

Yes, the good Doctor Reinhardt was involved in the Philadelphia Experiment. Dr. Reinhardt's involvement stemmed from one shared obsession: energy. The same energy he believed connected an ancient civilization, the infamous Hangar 51, and perhaps even alien technology.

This ancient power had something to do with crystals; " well, that's the way the ancient Egyptians and Atlanteans explained it", noted Dr. Thomas. And shortly after the Stealth Bomber was unveiled, new interest was generated in both Roswell and Hangar 51, the very same hangar from where aliens were purportedly kept and "studied". But the most fascinating idea that emerged from it all was the mention of an incredible power source—one generated by electricity, infused with magnetism, and capable of manipulating gravity itself.

You see, Dr. Reinhardt was very interested in the details of this article— not because he would benefit by it directly, but because he himself had worked with a very close friend – Dr. Einstein himself. It was Einstein who first told him about a secret project known only as "OPERATION RACEHORSE"!

SOMETHING WENT WRONG

Ensign Luke Wallace stood at the gangway as the "volunteer" crew boarded the USS ELDRIDGE, DD-273, medium-class destroyer. Some fifty sailors from various rates: sonar, radar, radio, engine, stores, navigation. Though they were volunteers, each had undergone extensive background checks. Not a stone was left unturned as to their pasts and their qualifications. Each had been trained in the latest research in acoustic sound waves, electromagnetic energy, propulsion, and radio wave propagation.

Captain A. T. Simons, skipper of the Eldridge, stood on the forecastle and surveyed the men as they came aboard. When all were "present and accounted for," he gave his first command, "Ensign, see to it that all gear is stowed below. Then, have the men report to the galley for a briefing. We depart tomorrow at 0200 hours."

"Aye, sir," the ensign replied and turned towards the sailors who were now standing silently at attention in a uniform group eagerly awaiting orders. Each of them wondered about the mission, what they would be doing, where they would be going and how they would contribute to the war effort. They were young, single, full of curiosity and ambitious.

Gunners Mate Splicy Thomson turned to Radioman Fred Norman and commented, "This sure is gonna be something. A secret mission. We don't get to do things like this down yonder in Arkansas." Norman shot back, "Neither do people from New York!"

The men filed down the ladder one by one to their berthing, emptied the contents of their sea bags onto their bunks, sorted and stowed their gear, then made their way to the galley. Once there, scrambled eggs, bacon, and pancakes were waiting for them. All were told to eat heartily. It was going to be a long day, and chow wouldn't be served again until 1300.

Exactly twenty minutes later, a tall, thin, executive type strode into the enlisted dining area. Someone shouted, "Attention on deck", and all hands snapped to attention. "As you were," Captain Simons said, stepping forward.

"Gentlemen," he began, "You have volunteered for a mission that is of the utmost importance to the security and war effort of your country. What you are about to embark on could not only turn the tide of the war in our favor, but it may tip the balance of power for decades to come and allow the United States to remain years after the war is over, as the most powerful nation on earth."

He added, "This experiment will test the limits of your professions, strengths, and devotion to the country. And, chances are, many of you will not survive. You have trained for months. Each one of you knows what to do and when to do it. We will not get any second chances. Perfection, from start to finish, is an absolute. Is that understood?"

The men stared at the captain in silence. Then, Chief Petty Officer Manuel Valenzuela barked, "Yes, sir" and the rest of the men followed suit in unison. The captain gave a few final words, "Very well men. We will commence operations at 0300. Ensign, make all preparations for getting underway at 0200 hours tomorrow. Chief, dismiss the crew to their duty stations."

Two weeks before, convoys of equipment under heavily guarded escort made their way from a secret location in the Pennsylvania countryside to the Philadelphia Naval shipyard and to "Pier 7, Berth 13". Security was so tight that nobody was allowed within a thousand yards of the ship unless authorized and under Marine escort.

First, six 500-kilowatt generators were installed on the main decks. Next, special wiring was placed throughout the Eldridge's thick internal bulkheads. The radio room was outfitted with a special control unit. The latest radar, sonar, and receivers were added. A sophisticated communications system utilizing a new voice-activated method was installed. Six Enormous, twenty feet by fifteen feet cylindrical magnetic generators were placed between the main electric generators. A foot thick copper cable ran from the main battery and generators to two main transformers located on the fantail. From there, they wound their way around the electro-magnetic generators and onto the main component, onto a large dish-shaped object located amidships, then placed on a turret so that the dish could rotate 360 degrees. In turn, additional one-foot-thick cables, more than 1000 feet of them, were wrapped around the Eldridge's hull. This in turn was connected to the electro-magnetic generators by four, foot-long coils.

The entire destroyer was transformed into what seemed to be a floating electrical substation that could probably supply all the power needed for Philadelphia for a year!

The sailors worked on through the wee hours of the morning. Shifts rotated so the work could continue nonstop. The men worked as a fine-tuned engine, never missing a beat. Their training and discipline had paid off. There was never a complaint, a lag in work, or a question offered up. Maybe it was because they themselves really didn't know what the assembly was really for, or they just wanted to make a difference in the war. No matter, they worked all through the morning up to midday without a hitch. There was a steady stream of gear coming and going throughout the ship and on board cranes lowered massive units of electrical components below decks. At 1300 hours, the crew broke for lunch. Thirty minutes later they were promptly back at their duty stations working as if they had never stopped.

The boatswain mate's whistle came over the loudspeaker at 1600 hours, and the chief's voice boomed over the squawk box, "Now hear this, now hear this. All hands secure from work details. Report to the mess hall at 1700 hours for chow and a brief. That is all."

The sailors finally showed some emotion as they were relieved from their duties. They all felt pretty good, having worked the entire day and outrigging their ship for its mission. Most of the work had been completed. From now on, it would be adding things here and there and testing all the systems. At 1700, the galley was alive and well with the clanking of metal trays on the rails sliding down the chow line and loud voices finally letting off steam. Men began to talk about home, their favorite baseball teams, and the war. Some bragged about a girlfriend here and there. And still others wondered out loud what their mission was, "Hey, Smalls, what do you suppose we are going to do?" Seaman Apprentice Wills asked Petty Officer Second Class Smalls. "Well, I reckon we have some secret laser that we are going to use against the Japanese or even Hitler himself. Like a ray gun." Everyone began to laugh out loud.

Little did they know that their laughs would soon turn into screams.

The Eldridge pulled out of its birth under the cover of fog and darkness the next day at 0200 hours. She did a silent five knots, trying not to leave a wake behind her. Her bow barely broke the serene waters of the calm bay. She steamed unnoticed and unchallenged out into the middle of the harbor, her crew making preparations for what was about to become the most coveted scientific experiment of all time.

Most of the crew were stunned when they came to a stop. They just looked at each other. And instead of using the squawk box to shout orders, each officer verbally told their units what to do and had each man pass the word along with a whisper. The sailors began to get a bit anxious as the Eldridge sat peacefully in the middle of the bay. The ship was darkened, and only a few red lights dimly showed the way down each passageway.

Across the bay two unidentified destroyers stood by, positioned as observers. Also present was an unexpected arrival of a merchant marine vessel, unaccounted for, that happened to be entering the harbor at the same time. One of the escorting destroyers signaled the vessel to hold its position and not approach. However, by the time she came to a full stop, she was already within 500 yards of the Eldridge's starboard side.

The Eldridge decreased her speed, then finally came to a halt. She sat majestically in the calm waters of the bay, silhouetted against the backdrop of the Philadelphia skyline. On either side, the observing destroyers had assumed their positions, flanking her at a distance of 100 yards to starboard and port.

At 0230 hours, a small launch could be seen approaching the Eldridge. Once alongside, the gang plank was lowered and three civilians were brought on board. An eyewitness from the merchant marine vessel, a sailor named Carl Allende, later recalled the moment in an interview,   "I recognized him from a photo in a book I was reading about physics. It was him, alright. I know we were still somewhat apart, but when they turned the light to shine on the gangplank and those three guys boarded, I was on watch and manning the binoculars from the port beam. I got more than a five-minute look at him. It was him! I'm sure of it. Nobody could ever mistake that mop of gray hair and the thick gray mustache; both stood out in the light's beam. It was Einstein!"

The two other men, Allende says, "were younger, like assistants, and carrying black like boxes and a briefcase. After a brief discussion with five or six officers and men, the three were lowered back into the launch and returned to the escort ship."

At 0250, the captain spoke to the crew on the ship's intercom. "This is the captain speaking. Radio, sonar, radar. Standby. Special Op room, standby to activate electrical impulse modulation. All hands to their stations. Check all coils, generators, and battery components. Prepare to start calibration and recording on my command. Stand by to commence **OPERATION RACEHORSE**! That is all."

The next twenty minutes saw the crew scurrying about, making sure all the equipment was in place and ready to go. However, the main area of importance was the Special Op room located next to the radio room. This is where Chief Petty Officer Bud Mowsely and Petty Officer Charles "Splicy" Price were checking the most important equipment on board.

"Splicey ole boy", Mowsely began. "If this goes the way it should, Dorothy and I will be walking down the Yellow Brick Road on the way to OZ!"

"Christ, Mows, check the goddamn equipment and make sure the readings are correct. I don't want to fry Toto the dog!"

Both were handpicked electronic warfare specialists trained to work on *new* pieces of equipment. They had been training under heavy security for the last eight months at a secret location somewhere in San Diego near the Navy's ASW school.

Mowsely carefully took the black box, unscrewed the four thumb screws, and opened the lid. Inside were two glass cylindrical objects, each resembling the likes of tubes found in the back of TV sets. The chief took both and inserted them into two round holes on the side of an instrument panel that was adorned with wires, lights, and dials. As soon as the tubes were secured, Petty Officer Splice opened the two notebooks and, referencing from both books, began to write some calculations down. He turned to a chart in the back of one of the notebooks and did a final equation. Next, he picked up the radio telephone and summoned the captain, "Special Op to Bridge. All is ready. Standing by." The captain came back immediately, "Very well. Standby." Then he called down to the radio room and ordered the following message sent to the observation ship off the port side. "Radio, send the following to designee; JULIET-OSCAR-CHARLIE-KILO-ECHO-YANKEE, **THE HORSES ARE IN THE GATES!**"

Aboard the unidentified escort vessel, the same message was relayed to Washington. Inside the Oval Office, President Roosevelt sat with his advisor, waiting nervously. Suddenly, an aide came in and announced, "Mr. President, message from STARTER: **THE HORSES ARE IN THE GATES.**"

President Roosevelt took a deep breath and softly exclaimed. "Well gentlemen, let's see if we can make a US NAVY warship disappear and reappear!" Everyone began to smile and cross their fingers.

Donovan's mind was racing when he finished the last sentence. He paused, drew in a breath, and finished up with the lead into the next part.

My faithful readers,

You are about to discover a chilling and almost unbelievable account of an event that took place aboard one of our own warships, deep within the circles of our military and government.

Donovan typed on through the night…

CHAPTER TEN

SOMETHING WENT WRONG

Donovan continued typing throughout the night and into the next morning…vowing not to stop until the series was completed…

…You could feel the excitement and anticipation in the captain's voice as he delivered the command everyone was waiting for.

"ATTENTION ALL CREW: STANDBY TO POWER UP ON MY COMMAND. RADIO, PASS TO COMMEASTFLT THE FOLLOWING MESSAGE: **THE FLAG IS UP**"

Mowsely looked at Splicy for an instant, nodded, and said, "Give her the juice Splice!"

He reached up above his head and grasped a silver and black knob. He turned it clockwise twice. Then, without letting go, he glanced down again at his notebook as if rechecking his calculations. Mowsely watched as the dials moved slowly, steadily upward. Splice began to call out the readings aloud, "twenty-five percent, fifty, eighty, ninety, hundred. Power complete skipper."

The captain gave the final order, "COMMENCE OPERATION. RADIO SEND FOLLOWING: **THEY'RE OFF AND RUNNING.**"

The generators were switched on, and the coils began to spin faster and faster. There was a powerful vibration that began to reverberate throughout the ship. Above decks, crewmen went about their jobs without hesitation, checking equipment, making sure coolant was flowing to the generators, and performing the other hundred or so duties that would make this operation a success. But the most important part of the experiment was going on below decks, where Mowsely and Splicy were assigned the most difficult tasks. They were the ones in charge of all the power.

Suddenly, Mowsely had a worried look on his face and asked in a panicked voice, "Jesus, Splice. Do math? What the hell is that vibration? Something wrong?"

Splice shot back an irritated glance and snapped, "It's the goddamn amount of power we have cooking. It's to be expected. Just watch the gauges and work the dam valves, Mowes."

A low, monotone humming sound came from the equipment. Splice turned the shiny dial again— two more times. He looked back up at his instruments and saw that a small meter showed the numbers: 100% power reading for all generators. All coils except for one at max *RPMs*. This one was past its max rpm rating and steadily rotating faster. Reports from topside said the vibration was getting worse, the decks were getting too hot to stand on, and the noise was almost unbearable.

Splicy called up to the bridge and gave his report. Speaking in a trained, vigilant tone, he began, "Captain, all systems are a go. Power levels at plus 100. Electromagnetic pulses holding steady at 2.2 cycles per second. The molecular reorganization sequence has been initialized.

Coil number three, *RPMs* exceeding max by 2x. Standing by for full generator power up, sir. Awaiting further orders."

There was no hesitation on the other end. The captain's voice came booming through the radio telephone, "CONTINUE OP, POWER TO MAX CYCLES."

Splicey had anticipated the captain commenting on the *RPMs* and came back with a request, "Captain, the *RPMs* of coil 3 are max plus 2x. They are increasing, but at a slow rate."

"CONTINUE OP. I REPEAT, CONTINUE OP. POWER TO MAX CYCLES AND COMMENCE OPERATION OF DEVICE."

Splice froze for an instant then turned the knob to his highest position.

The entire deck of the Eldridge started to shake. Her hull shuddered and she heaved from starboard to port, and her bow dipped hard into the calm bay and came back up again. The crew scurried to control the situation, but too many things were happening too fast, and each movement and incident was too overwhelming to deal with.

A shudder and loud vibration could be felt and heard throughout the Eldridge. The entire crew became silent and helplessly awaited the outcome. The vibrations grew stronger. Within fifteen minutes, the electro-magnetic generators were producing gigawatts of electricity. Suddenly, anything metal that was not bolted down began to be pulled towards the magnetic coils. Without warning, a surge of electricity surged throughout the ship, knocking all hands off their feet. Small explosions erupted and fires started to break out below decks. The men began to scream as the electric current surged through their bodies.

Another several agonizing minutes passed, and the Eldridge was surrounded in a greenish hue. Its hull continued to vibrate, and then new screams resounded throughout the ship, "I'm burning!", "It's cold!", "The other side. I can see it!", "It's all black, frozen here! Help me! Oh God!"

It was terrible, chaotic, and horrific.

Down in Spec Ops, Splicey and Mowsely tried in vain to shut off the power. "Goddamn it Splice! What the hell is going on?! Turn the…" Just then a million-plus volts, mixed with magnetic impulses took Mowsely by surprise. At first, his hands and legs became rigid. Then, his eyes grew wide and went white. His whole body began to "MELT, or BREAK APART"; it just DISSOLVED right into the deck! Blood, muscle, brain, skin, all turned to liquid, leaving the odor of death behind. Splicey was screaming into the sound-powered phone, "Captain! He's gone! I can't turn off the power! Help!" But it was too late. Splicey became the next victim of the "experiment", one that was playing out exactly as the Navy had predicted it would.

On the escort vessels, you could see the crews scurrying at the command of "RESCUE! RESCUE!" Lifeboats could be seen being lowered into the bay, and signal lights could be seen communicating between the two escort vessels. Contact tried to be established with the Eldridge, but it was to no avail. In the control room of one of the observation ships, a sailor manning the radar cried out, "SIR, THE ELDRIDGE IS OFF THE SCREEN! SHE'S VANISHED, SIR! ALL OBSERVATION POSTS AFLOAT AND ASHORE REPORT NO BLIPS OR SIGHTINGS SIR."

"WAIT, STANDBY…A MESSAGE FROM ATLANTIC FLEET HEADQUARTERS COMING IN….MESSAGE READS…DESTROYER, DD-173 SPOTTED 2 MILES OFF VIRGINIA COAST…HULL IDENTIFIED. THAT IS ALL."

MISSION ACCOMPLISHED!

The President could only listen in horror as the squawk box played out a nightmare in the making. Roosevelt began to mumble to himself, *"It was so easy! The vortices, the magnetic net, the resultant forces that hold objects in place, as to 'transfer' their properties – molecules and atoms."*

He stared blankly ahead, voice low and haunted. "The entire process was to take only thirty minutes. Turn the voltage up, turn the electromagnets on, feed in a second high-energy current, and that's it. Amazing! A cloaking device. A year-long scientific theory of quantities and tensor equations and endless combinations and, well, we did it! Well, HE did it! Einstein's predictions of 1927 came true.

His UNIFIED THEORY and ELECTROMAGNETISM have just become a reality. But, I'm afraid the rest of his predictions may come true as well - killing mankind."

But on this day, the electric and magnetic fields that were created within the massive coiling system went, in layman's terms, "crazy", or "haywire". Current surged throughout the entire ship, sending billions of volts and unmeasurable amounts of energy, and God only knows what else, through the bodies of human beings that caused suffering beyond imagination.

Back in Philadelphia, the two escort ships made full steam towards the Eldridge, or where they THOUGHT the Eldridge was. As they approached the area, all that could be seen was that same greenish, glowing "mist" as it was described by witnesses, glowing with clouds encircling the area and leftover electrical charges still shooting across the water, accompanied by what sounded like mini sounds of short-circuiting and claps of thunder. Both observation ships' instruments began to go awry, and both skippers ordered their vessels to go DEAD IN THE WATER.

For what felt like an eternity—but was only a matter of minutes—the bay remained still, empty, and eerily quiet. Then, through the lingering mist, the faint outline of a hull began to shimmer back into view, some hundred yards away. A lookout's voice pierced the silence.

"Destroyer, 2 o'clock!"

When the ships reached the Eldridge, her entire hull and deck were charred. Bodies, half bodies, could be seen lying on the deck or actually immersed in the bulkheads! Hands, feet, arms, and legs were missing from several of the men. Some survivors were moaning in pain, rambling on about strange noises, beings, darkness, bright lights, going somewhere else; it was all too confusing and horrible to make any sense of it all. One sailor, burnt beyond recognition, sat rigid and kept repeating, "I saw a bright light. I saw God. Well, it may have been God. I don't know.

I was outside my body. I was hovering over the ship. I was outside my body. I saw God."

It was a dreadful scene. The entire bay was closed off, and tug boats came out and towed the Eldridge back to its secure berthing. Fifteen survivors were taken to an emergency medical facility under heavy guard in an abandoned hangar.

Back in Washington, President Roosevelt wiped a tear from his eye, stood up, strode toward the window, and looked out onto the White House lawn. He said simply, humbly, quietly, "SOMETHING WENT WRONG."

Yes, THE PHILADELPHIA EXPERIMENT DID TAKE PLACE AND IT WAS A MISERABLE FAILURE. HOWEVER, IT AWOKE THE WORLD TO WHAT PHYSICS AND SCIENCE CAN REALLY DO WHEN PUT TO THE TEST. THE EFFECTS ON THE CREW WERE DEVASTATING AND THEIR WHEREABOUTS ARE UNKNOWN UNTIL THIS DAY. RUMORS ABOUND ABOUT GOVERNMENT COVER-UPS AND CONTEMPORARY INTERVENTION BY RUSSIAN SCIENTISTS ON THE VERY TOPIC.

So, what do YOU, the readers, think? Did it happen? Where are the volunteers? Was there a government cover-up? Will we ever know the truth? Is there a connection between aliens and the Philadelphia Experiment? Or, is this just another glorified hoax?

To this day, our military vehemently denies ever taking part in such an operation or ever working with Dr. Einstein.

End of Part III. End Series.

Dr. Reinhardt set the copy of the San Diego Herald down on his desk. As he did, his face became distorted, and he began to weep out loud, "What did we do? Oh God! We crossed the line!"

Just as he spoke these words, the doorbell rang. And as if already knowing what was about to happen, Dr. Reinhardt got up, walked to the door and slowly turned the knob. Not surprised in the least, he looked up at the three men in black suits. Breaking the silence, he remarked, "Well, nobody expected to keep this a secret forever."

As he spoke these last words, one of the men revealed the barrel of a .22 caliber silencer. Dr. Reinhardt lowered his head and closed his eyes.

CHAPTER ELEVEN

SEPARATE WORK FROM PLAY

Donovan's heart was pounding as he finished the last words and set the manuscript down. "My God…. Did I just write that?" he asked himself.

Donovan was done! Now he waited…

In what seemed to be an eternity, within twenty minutes of the first of the morning papers having been delivered, the phone rang. It was Cid. "Coach! You did it! You hella did it! And, you got your first reaction."

Donovan asked, "How's that?"

"Christ Coach, Dr. Reinhardt is dead - murdered!"

Donovan shot back, "Well Cid, I hope you're happy. I can't wait until they come and get ME!"

Donovan no sooner hung up when there was a knock on the apartment door. Donovan slowly, cautiously, cracked the door open, leaving the safety chain still attached. He peered through the small opening. He froze. His heart stopped. He just stared. He could not mutter a sound. His face became ashen, and his body went numb. The last person in the world he would expect to ever come back into his life was now gazing at him. A short-haired, blue-eyed woman, 35 years of age, a bit over 5ft 2in, calmly spoke, "Preevet Misha moj. Kak dela? Hello my Misha. How are you?"

Nobody had called Donovan "Misha" since his days as a Russian linguist in the Navy. The last person to call him that was his lost love, the one now standing at the door - Dawn Metzger. Better known to him as "Dasha".

Dasha came from a German-Russian background. Her mother was a professor at Moscow State University and her father was a dentist. Both were hardworking loyal Communists. Her father, Hans Metzger had grown up in what was then, East Germany. He was raised under the Soviet yoke and hated every moment of it. However, Dasha's mom was a member of the Communist party, and yet fell for this gentle caring, broad shouldered Bavarian man.

Dasha had gone to MGU (Moscow State University) and had been recruited by the KGB because of her high scores in political and international studies. She learned English and spoke three other languages. She was responsible, quick-minded, and flirtatious - a mix of much-needed Soviet needs.

She and Donovan, "MISHA", met when Dasha was in the Republic of Georgia, at a cafe in the capital, Tbilisi. Misha had been assigned to monitor Soviet ground forces and the response to Georgian protests and efforts to secure their independence. Misha had befriended a Georgian underground contact, a woman known only as "Maria". Misha lived in the basement of her flat. Maria and her two children occupied the main floor. Together, they collected intel and passed it on to CIA operatives working outside of Tbilisi. They made a good team, and after working together for three months, Misha was in the house when a small boy asked him to help a neighbor start his car. He soon left the house when an explosion leveled the house. Misha barely escaped with his life.

Dasha had a deep hatred towards the KGB and was well-versed in Western life. She began to change her views and approached the CIA operatives. She became a double agent and began working with Misha and other CIA agents within the republic.

"Dasha, it has been a long time. I still owe you my life for sending that boy to the house to make me come outside and help Pyotr start his car. It was sad to see Maria and her children killed."

"Da Misha. Terrible, Uzhasno." Dasha replied.

"You told me you loved me, Dasha. You said we would 'sail away somewhere on the Black Sea someday.' But NO! You left me standing there on the street. You looked back at me as you got into a small black car and vanished. The next thing I knew I was picked up by a "taxi" and whisked away. I was told to leave and given a backpack and directions. I walked for days until I got to the ocean and was picked up by a fisherman who took me to Rize, Turkey, on to Sinop, then back to Rota, Spain. And, now, you are here at my door!"

Dasha's eyes met Misha's. Her blue eyes teared up. "Misha moj, my Misha, I NEVER, EVER LEFT! I was with you this entire time, but I could not tell you the truth. I had a duty to my mission. I, too, was assigned to find out about the Philadelphia Experiment. I too was to find out about this power source. I spent years learning the history of the USS ELDRIDGE DD-213. This research took me all over the world. I ended up in Greece, where the Eldridge was berthed in Crete. It was missing the log book for 1943 and had been reconfigured to carry some kind of equipment. The mounts were still there, but there was no equipment. I managed to become part of a refit crew and found strange wiring inside the ship. There were burn marks and scratches on the bulkheads. That was it. Then, they said you were in trouble, and I got you out of Georgia. From there, I have monitored your every move. Cid has kept me updated. And the cars that have occasionally been parked at the top of the hill by Mast Bridge, by West Hills - I was in all of them, watching you go to work. Do you know how I wanted to talk to you, to hold you?" Donovan just stared back in disbelief when Dasha screamed, "DURAK MISHA! STUPID MISHA! I know everything you have been doing. You started researching this while in the Navy. I know about the letter you wrote Berlitz, and I know he wrote you back. He was the leading authority on the Philadelphia Experiment. He, too, was silenced. You wrote letters to the Navy and they denied everything. You wrote to Einstein's lawyer, and he too denied everything. And, HE TOO IS NOT WITH US ANYMORE! I know about your run-in with security at Area 51. The only reason you were not shot is because we have an agent on the inside. I was able to warn him in time."

She paused, her voice steady but laced with something deeper—regret, maybe.

She looked Donovan in the eye. "I had no choice because I also work for CID, "retired" CIA. And he works for Kuznetsov, and Kuznetsov is my Uncle!" The weight of the truth hung between them.

She stepped closer, softer now. "Ultimately, we needed someone to see this Steinmetz article through and finish it. And who better than you? A former spook, a teacher, and a would-be Pulitzer Prize dreamer." She held his gaze.

"But this is the end, Misha. It is almost over."

A pause. Then softer— "Trust me."

Misha didn't hesitate. He stepped forward, wrapped his arms around Dasha, and kissed her—deeply, urgently, like time itself had been holding its breath. When they parted, he whispered, "Okay, khorosho, okay. What is next?"

Dasha's expression turned serious. "We wait for THEIR move."

Misha frowned, eyes narrowing and confused, "Their? Who are *they*?"

Just then, a car pulled up and screeched to a halt. Dasha grabbed Misha by the arm and pushed him sideways. She revealed a 9mm Beretta and, without hesitation, opened fire, hitting the driver with the first shot and sending the car into a retaining wall. "Suk ee sini, sons of bitches have found us! Let's go Mish…. make like you're going for three and hall ass. And here, remember how to use this?" She tossed him a .45 she had in her coat pocket.

"Yea." "Then start shooting!" Within a few moments, three men dressed in black suits lay bloody, dead on the pavement. The duo fled down a back alley and across Santee Lakes.

Soon, they were strolling along the shore. Donovan told Dasha, "From now on we use our professional names, Mike Donovan and Dawn Metzger." Dasha's eyes glared at Donovan, and she sarcastically shot back, "Sure thing, coach!" But Donovan was angry. He wanted to know what the hell was going on, "Goddamn it Dawn. Who are these people? FBI? CIA? FSB? old KGB? Who? Kto? Skazhi mne! Tell me!"

Dasha stopped, turned to Donovan, smiled, and replied, "Misha, let's go to your boat. I have never made love on a boat."

CHAPTER TWELVE

HEADING FOR HOME

Michael Donovan became "Misha". Dawn Metzger became "Dasha". Great cover names for two people who had always wanted to be more than themselves. Since they first met, both had had the same desire to be someone special, to give back to the country where their parents had done so much for, and their family histories played such a vital role in their own development. Being together again on the one hand was exciting and unpredictable, on the other it felt empty, depressing, and frightening. However, it didn't take long for the two to cut through all the years of "what ifs" and bond together again, as if they had never been apart.

The sun was barely rising, casting its reflective light on the serenity of San Diego Bay. Donovan emerged from the cabin of the Pelican Watch, a beautiful forty-foot Grand Banks Yacht he and his father had purchased together. It had become more than just a boat—it was home. Donovan took up residence on the boat, and weekends were spent fishing the Coronado Islands or cruising up the coast to La Jolla. Often, Donovan would come down the docks ready to relax after a long day at school, only to find his father, a retired WWII pilot and mechanic, below decks working on the engines, with parts and gear spread out all over the deck.

As "skip", as Donovan was called while on the boat, emerged from below decks, he found Dawn sitting in one of the captain's chairs on the fantail, sipping coffee and admiring the beauty of the marina. She could see the carriers across at North Island Naval Base standing out over everything else on the bay.

As Donovan approached Dawn, their eyes met. Both began to speak at the same time,

"How are you this…." Dawn smiled, and Donovan sat next to her and softly kissed her forehead.

Donovan took over the conversation., "Well, if you feel the same way I do this morning then you'll want to take this boat to sea, leave all this behind us and never come back. Besides, isn't this what we planned many years ago?"

"I do", Dawn replied. "But first, you need to know the entire truth. The whole story. And then, we need to contact some people here and make things happen. I have already started this process for us. As we speak, Cid is in Washington. From there, he is headed to Moscow to meet with my uncle. Let's hope he accomplishes his mission. As he always has told me, 'loyal to the cause until the end. No matter the price." But first, read this. It will explain everything. Most of it will be a shock to you. And remember, I have been by your side this entire time." She handed him a classified report, marked "Top Secret. Codeword - **PRAVDA** (TRUTH). "Most is in Russian, but there are notes in English in the margins. It was written by my uncle years ago and submitted to the KGB. He was held responsible for so many secrets. You will understand once you read everything. Here, sit down, Misha…."

OPERATSIA RAZGOVOR
(OPERATION CONVERSATION)

TRANSLATOR'S NOTE: TRANSLATED BY A. V. KUZNETSOV FSB INTEL CODE 42

ORIGIN OF MATERIAL - 1942

THIS DOCUMENT IS A SUMMARY OF EVENTS THAT BEGAN WITH THE NKVD AND TRANSFERRED TO KGB FILES WITH THE ADVENT OF THE KGB IN 1953 AND SUBSEQUENTLY TO THE FSB WITH THE FALL OF THE SOVIET UNION.

THE SOVIET GOVERNMENT HAS BEEN MONITORING THE SCIENTIST, DR EINSTEIN, AND HIS WORK WITH A NEW FOUND ENERGY. OUR OPERATIVES HAVE BEEN WORKING WITH HIGH-LEVEL NAVAL OFFICERS THAT ARE WILLING TO SHARE THIS INFORMATION UNDER THE PREMISE OF ENDING THE WAR SOONER VIA A JOINT EFFORT, ONE IN WHICH WASHINGTON REFUSES TO ACKNOWLEDGE. WE ALSO HAVE RUMORS OF UFO ACTIVITY AND A SECRET BASE CALLED AREA 51.

IN 1942, THERE WAS A REPORT OF A UFO CRASH IN THE SIBERIAN WILDERNESS NEAR THE SMALL TOWN OF "EYIK". SOVIET SCIENTISTS WERE QUICKLY DISPATCHED AND A TEAM NOT ONLY FOUND "UNEARTHLY OBJECTS", BUT THEY FOUND THAT EINSTEIN'S THEORY OF RELATIVITY "IS APPLICABLE TO THIS SITUATION" (CLASSIFICATION - HIGH CODE 45 AND NOT MEANT FOR THIS DOCUMENT). BUT SEVERAL SCIENTISTS WERE ABLE TO "ASSEMBLE SOME EQUIPMENT AT A LAB IN MOSCOW AND MAKE SOME OBJECTS APPEAR AND REAPPEAR IN A VACUUM. (AGAIN CLASSIFICATION - HIGH CODE 45 AND NOT MEANT FOR THIS DOCUMENT).

THIS ENTIRE PROJECT WAS ORDERED BY STALIN, BUT WHEN HE DIED ON MARCH 5, 1953, ACTIVITIES WERE HALTED. AS STALIN'S OWN NOTES DESCRIBE, "WE ARE NEARLY IN THE GRASP OF THE TRUTH TO PREVENT UNFORESEEABLE CATASTROPHE WITH THE USE OF THIS POWER, COMBINED WITH THE EVENTUAL DISCOVERY OF NUCLEAR WEAPONS, WHICH EINSTEIN HIMSELF FEARED."

ON SEPT 19, 1959, KRUSHCHEV VISITED DISNEYLAND. A YOUNG SENATOR NAMED KENNEDY HAD A SECRET MEETING WITH KRUSHCHEV. DURING THIS MEETING, KENNEDY PROMISED KRUSHCHEV THAT WHEN HE BECAME PRESIDENT, THIS POWER WOULD BE A JOINT VENTURE TO "PURSUE ITS CAPABILITY IN ORDER TO MAINTAIN WHAT WE WILL SOMEDAY NEED TO SECURE THE FUTURE OF THE WORLD'S SURVIVAL - MUTUAL DETERRENCE."

KENNEDY WOULD THEN OFFER KHRUSHCHEV THIS VERY FORMULA FOR DETERRENCE.

ALL THIS WAS TO TAKE PLACE OVER THE NEXT SEVERAL YEARS. HOWEVER, THE CUBAN MISSILE CRISIS PREEMPTED THIS ENDEAVOR AND IT FADED AWAY COMPLETELY WITH KENNEDY'S ASSASSINATION,UNDENIABLY, BY SHALL WE SAY, "MUTUAL PARTNERSHIPS".

THE FORMULA FOR THIS POWER TO MAKE SHIPS, WEAPONS, OTHER EQUIPMENT, DISAPPEAR AND REAPPEAR IN ORDER TO EVADE TIMELY DETECTION, WOULD PROVE SUPERIOR IN THE EVENT OF WAR. HOWEVER, IN THE HANDS OF A ROGUE NATION COULD WREAK UNIMAGINABLE HAVOC ON MANKIND. THEREFORE, THE CREATION OF JOINT US/SOVIET PERSONNEL TO OVERSEE THE DEMISE OF THIS PROGRAM AND ITS PROGRESS IS TANTAMOUNT

TO THE SECURITY OF ALL NATIONS. IN JOINT RESPONSE, WE WILL ERADICATE ALL EVIDENCE OF THE SO-CALLED POWER AND THE EVENT ENTITLED **"THE PHILADELPHIA EXPERIMENT"**, AS WELL AS MAKING SURE THAT ALL THOSE INVOLVED ARE COMMITTED TO THE APPROPRIATE INSTITUTIONS. THIS "JOINT" COMMITTEE WILL ALSO BE IN CHARGE OF ALL POLITICAL AND MILITARY COMMUNICATION WITH THE PUBLIC TO PUT TO REST ANY CURIOSITY OF THE MATTER. IN THE BETTER SENSE OF THE WORD, IT SHALL DENY ANY OF THIS EVER TOOK PLACE. WITH THIS STATED AND ACCORDING TO ALL DIRECTIVES, A SYSTEMATICAL MONITORING OF THIS SHALL COMMENCE AND WILL SUBSEQUENTLY BE INTEGRATED INTO ALL FUTURE DEALINGS. OPERATIVES WILL BE EMPOWERED TO TERMINATE AT WILL ANY AND ALL WHO ARE AFFILIATED OR ATTEMPT TO BE AFFILIATED IN ANY WAY WITH THE PHILADELPHIA PROJECT, ITS PROPERTIES, AND ANY PURSUIT OF ANY SCIENTIFIC STUDIES TO THE AFOREMENTIONED NARRATIVE.

Donovan could not believe his eyes. He was stunned, gripping the papers tighter and tighter as he read, becoming more frustrated by the minute. He thought, "This is why everyone associated with this project has vanished or died: Morris Jessup, Steinmetz, the Senator, the ATC personnel, Holland, and - Christ! We are probably next."

The report continues.....

THERE IS ONE OTHER SITUATION THAT IS CRUCIAL THAT INVOLVES AN EYE WITNESS. THERE

WAS A MERCHANT MARINE VESSEL ANCHORED IN PHILADELPHIA HARBOR. THIS WAS THE ORIGINAL CARGO SHIP, THE "MARCO POLO". THIS VESSEL WAS 'NEUTRALIZED'. SHORTLY AFTER WITNESSING THE ELDRIDGE DISAPPEAR AND THEN REAPPEAR, IT HEADED OUT TO SEA. SHORTLY THEREAFTER, THERE WAS AN EXPLOSION ON BOARD THE FREIGHTER. THE MARCO POLO SANK WITHIN MINUTES WITH ALL 26 CREWMEMBERS GOING DOWN WITH THE SHIP, EXCEPT ONE, A MAN NAMED CARL ALLENDE, WHO WAS STANDING THE STERN WATCH. REPORTS SURFACED THAT HE WITNESSED EINSTEIN COMING ABOARD THE ELDRIDGE FOR 'ABOUT AN HOUR', THEN LEAVING TO A SHORE OBSERVATION POST, ACCOMPANIED WITH HIGH-RANKING NAVAL OFFICERS AND OTHER CIVILIANS.

IN THE LATE 50'S, ALLENDE SURFACED IN LECTURE HALLS AND UFO CONVENTIONS AS A SELF-PROCLAIMED EXPERT. HE BEGAN SHARING HIS STORY AS THE ONLY WITNESS OF THE PHILADELPHIA EXPERIMENT. INTERESTINGLY ENOUGH, HE HAD SOME INCREDIBLE DETAILS THAT WERE EITHER JUST MADE-UP LIES, OR, THE TRUTH!

MOST PEOPLE THINK HE IS NUTS, EXCEPT THE "COMMITTEE, MADE UP OF THE CHOSEN, JOINT KGB (NOW FSB) AND CIA PERSONNEL. HE EVEN MADE CONTACT WITH SOME SURVIVORS 'IN A HOSPITAL', THE LATTER ALL SUCCUMBING TO VARIOUS ILLNESSES. HE WAS CLOSE TO ONE OF THE SURVIVORS, AN ALAN HUMES, WHO ESCAPED. THE ONLY PARTICIPANT IS ALLENDE AS HE PROFESSES. BUT ALAN DID SURFACE AND DID TRY TO TELL HIS STORY. BUT AT 80 AND SUFFERING FROM SEIZURES, PEOPLE WROTE HIM OFF AS A NUTCASE. BUT THE

DETAILS THAT HE TOO TOLD WERE TOO MUCH TO IGNORE. BUT THE STORY GETS DEEPER…

THE ARTICLES THAT STEINMETZ WAS WORKING ON WERE BASED ON A MEETING THAT ALAN HAD WITH THE WRITER AT SOME POINT AND, IN THE BOOK 'THE FIFTEEN MISSING MEN' (IN KUZNETSOV'S POSSESSION), IT TELLS MUCH OF THE SAME STORY. AND THIS VERY BOOK WAS WRITTEN BY ALAN HUMES, ALIAS BRAD WYMAN. THE BOOK WAS DICTATED TO AN UNKNOWN AUTHOR AND SELF-PUBLISHED.

THE USSR/RUSSIAN FEDERATION AND THE UNITED STATES JOINTLY CONTROL THIS 'CLOAKING DEVICE'. THE GOAL TODAY IS FOR MUTUAL DETERRENCE BETWEEN THE TWO POWERS AND THE EFFORT TO KEEP IT FROM GETTING INTO THE WRONG HANDS. DETERRENCE MUST BE MAINTAINED 'AT ALL COSTS'.

Donovan tossed the papers to the floor in disgust. "So nobody is safe. Nobody cares. We are all sacrificed for the survival of the world." Dawn shot back, "Ah, but didn't your President Roosevelt say the same thing after Pearl Harbor?"

CHAPTER THIRTEEN

AND THE WINNER IS

Cid was visiting old friends in Washington, trying to make an effort to contact members of the "committee" in order to stop the turn of events. At the same time, he tried to find out if anything was connected to Admiral Hollin's suicide. For some unknown reason he was given a warm welcome by old friends and after several weeks of prodding he was on the brink of a huge breakthrough, having discovered a rare circulated copy of a book, entitled, **COMMANDER X**. This was considered to be the bible of the Philadelphia Experiment, revealing its participants, anyone who attempted to write any non-fictional piece about it, or "experts" on the subject. It talks about a group of people who "carried out all the necessary means to silence all efforts to allow this measure to go forth in any way."

During these weeks, Donovan went back to the classroom and maintained his low profile. Splitting time between his apartment and the boat, he took to writing letters again to hospitals, the government, and other entities, trying to find out what happened to the brave Navy sailors who risked their lives. A few days went by, and Dawn returned to the boat with a sad look on her face. When he asked what was wrong, she simply replied, "My uncle," she said quietly, "informed me that all those involved in the Experiment had been terminated, the last one… died five years ago. The only person left with any connection to the project, this so-called Allende, is still missing."

Donovan felt the air leave the room. There was another issue. Her uncle was now missing, and all inquiries fell on deaf ears. He had worked behind the scenes in Moscow to smuggle the book out to Cid. He did his own digging using his trusted sources and research he had been compiling at the Admiralty in St Petersburg. Then, on a Saturday afternoon, having just exited his hotel, located across from the battleship Aurora, a car pulled up and he was arrested by the local *militsiya*. He was taken to the airport, put on a private jet, flown to Moscow, and taken to Lefortovo Prison in Moscow. After days of interrogation, he was given a speedy trial and sentenced to twenty years hard labor. When friends and family tried to contact the penal colony in the Urals where he was sent, the only reply they received was, "No such inmate exists here."

Dasha leaned her head on Misha's shoulder and began to cry. "Why, Misha? Pochemu?"

"Because it has always been this way. Anyone connected. Remember?"

"Misha!"

The two put the canvas cover on the flybridge and decided to go for a walk.

Cid had been in Moscow for a week and saw Kuznetsov right before he was arrested. The two were taking part in the post Soviet frenzy of the new "freedom". They visited places that had previously been off limits for some 70 years and celebrated at some of the local bars, engaging in conversations that just a year before would have brought someone a ten-year sentence in the Gulag. Cid bid farewell and flew to Washington. Oddly, it was right after he left Moscow that Kuznetsov was arrested. Cid never knew.

In Washington, he met with the son of the late Admiral Hollins, who had tragically died in a car accident shortly after he met with Allende, who had given a speech about the Philadelphia Experiment in 1957. Hollins had gathered information and was close to knowing the truth. He was on his way to Naval Intelligence when the "accident" occurred.

Cid was able to get some of his old buddies on Capitol Hill to start an inquiry into what had taken place over the years; the many deaths, missing navy personnel, government officials, Russian intervention and the discovery of some major documents he had recently come across which were tucked away in the Area 51 archives.

On an early Friday morning some two weeks later a very frail, short elderly man came walking down the dock headed for the Pelican Watch. He had his hands in his pockets, looking down. Donovan saw him coming and had a sick, yet curious feeling, muttering to himself, "Jesus, could this be HIM?"

The man stopped at the foot of the gangway and looked up. "Hello, Mr. Donovan. Or should I call you 'Misha'? My name is Allen Humes."

Donovan wasn't surprised at all. "Hello, Mr. Humes. I sort of knew you'd be coming around. What can I do for you?"

He sat on the deck bench, hands trembling slightly. "I am here to tell you the truth. To tell you everything. You are my last listener. And, I know YOU WILL believe me. You see, they did terrible things to us during the Experiment. When the motors were turned on and the magnetism was turned up. We all felt a terrible vibration, and a sensation that felt like our brains were collapsing from the outside in. For a moment, I looked down and my legs were gone - then they came back. Some of my friends just vanished before my eyes. Others came and went. And still others, like Splicey, my best friend, came from the engine room, and he was a 'ghost'! " Donovan stayed silent, jaw tight.

"It was horrible. For what seemed to be an eternity, we were looking out over a different bay, with lights shining on us. There were flashes and a greenish glow all around. Then, we were 'back'. Well, a few of us were. About 15 of us. They hauled us all to a mental facility in Colorado. Some died, some committed suicide, others were given an overdose of morphine and opioids until they overdosed and past. and still others, hung on. Like me. I was lucky. I left in a laundry cart one morning."

Donovan could not believe his ears. But he had read and researched so much, and he knew this was the truth. And, it WAS the same material from the book, **Commander X**! And we knew now that it was Alan Humes who began writing this book! But there was no proof, until Humes handed a worn-out photo to Donovan.

"Look at this", Humes began. "The photo is dated 1943 on the back. Check it yourself. It is the Eldridge, clear, its hull number 213 on the bow. This was taken by Carl Allende on the Marco Polo. It is the only piece of evidence. The photo captures the light flashes, the glow, and men frozen in place on the deck. Some are lying down, some are standing. You can tell things are not good. Carl gave me this picture right before HE was killed last month."

Allen nodded his head, turned and disappeared into the morning fog down the walkway and headed to the parking lot.

The next day, Donovan made copies of the photo and FedExed them to various government and military agencies as well as to the Russian Federation and the FSB, hoping that the photo would help preserve mutual deterrence. Following the "proof," several high government officials and military personnel in both countries were brought in for "questioning".

In January of 1993 President Clinton held a top secret meeting with his Chiefs of Staff, informing them that the United States in cooperation with the Russian Federation, upon acquiring new found proof and interviewing many in both countries, have made some startling discoveries that showed that some type of secret activity based on an "unnatural power" had taken place in

1943, involving the Navy. From this time on, the security of this episode and the potential risks it would have on mankind had to be contained. In addition, we must honor all those who have given their lives to the preservation of our country, our world, our very existence. We especially honor the volunteers who gave their lives undergoing this gruesome experiment that took place on the USS ELDRIDGE, DD-213. The fifteen men now deemed, MIA, or Missing in Action, will be honored with the highest military honors, " having perished during military operations behind enemy lines sometime between January 1942 and June 1944.

They are as follows; Chief Petty Officer Splicey…..”

On May 4, 1997, Dasha and Misha were married in the beautiful cathedral of Svetitskhovel in the small town of Mtsketa, in the Republic of Georgia.

Misha and Dasha sailed away from the small town of Poti on the Black Sea coast in July of 97. There has been no trace of them since.

The End.